A Twist of Malice

A
Twist
of
Malice

Jean Rae Baxter

SERAPHIM EDITIONS

Library and Archives Canada Cataloguing in Publication

Baxter, Jean Rae
     A twist of malice / Jean Rae Baxter.

ISBN 0-9734588-4-4

     I. Title.

PS8603.A935T85 2005   C813'.6   C2005-904544-2

Editor: Kerry J. Schooley
Cover and Interior Design: Marijke Friesen
Cover Image: Janice Jackson
Author photo: Today's Faces Photography

The publisher gratefully acknowledges the financial assistance of The Canada Council for the Arts and The Ontario Arts Council.

Printed and bound in Canada

Seraphim Editions
238 Emerald Street North
Hamilton, Ontario
Canada L8L 5K8
info@seraphimeditions.com

ONTARIO ARTS COUNCIL
CONSEIL DES ARTS DE L'ONTARIO

Canada Council
for the Arts

Conseil des Arts
du Canada

For John

No words enough to say my thanks

Table of Contents

Depression Glass

"Connie, you never had a child."

"Oh, but I did," said Connie. Her teacup rattled on the saucer when she picked it up. "I just never told you. I never told anyone before."

"Now, Connie …" Gertrude began, but did not continue. She did not like the tone she heard in her own voice—a scolding tone. Bite your tongue, Gertrude! she said to herself. She picked up a biscuit from the plate on the coffee table and nibbled at it, keeping her eyes on her sister's face.

Connie was smiling, her clouded blue eyes gazing across the room at the pattern of lace curtains cast by afternoon sunshine against the parlour wall. What was she seeing? Surely not the shadow of lace or the faded bird-of-paradise wallpaper! With her cup of tea suspended halfway to her lips,

Connie looked as if she had fallen into a trance. Apart from the trembling of her hand, she was as motionless as a statue. Gertrude was considering whether she ought to get up and take the teacup from her, when Connie spoke again.

"1931."

"What about 1931?"

"That was the year my little girl was born." Connie turned her head and looked at Gertrude. Apparently remembering the cup of tea in her hand, Connie raised it the rest of the way to her lips, took a sip, and then lowered the cup to her saucer.

For a few moments Gertrude could think of nothing to say. Of course Connie had not had a child, not in 1931 or any other year! The idea was ridiculous.

"Weren't you working in Ben Markham's office in 1931?" said Gertrude.

"Yes," said Connie. "As a stenographer. My first job. I was eighteen and very happy to have work, when many others had none."

"I remember how excited you were when Mr. Markham gave you the job," said Gertrude. "And how surprised."

Shy, gentle Connie had been so nervous about her job interview that she threw up on her new pleated skirt and had to change before she could leave the house. But somehow she had survived the ordeal.

Five years later, Mr. Markham fired her when she asked for a raise. Connie never tried that again. For the next forty-five years she worked in one small office after another, demanding nothing. Then she retired to take care of Mother. That was the story of Connie's life.

She had never done anything. Never travelled. Never married. Never even had a beau. She had lived in this shabby little house all her life, or at least since she was six years old. That was when Father bought it.

And now Connie lived in a world of memories. In itself, that was no problem. Gertrude did the same. When you're close to ninety years old, what other world do you have?

The problem was that most of Connie's memories were fantasies. Some were made-up stories of things that had never happened. Others were of things that really had happened, but to somebody else. The trip to England, for example. Last week, when Gertrude came for her usual Tuesday afternoon visit, Connie told her about a wonderful trip to England, with all sorts of details about Wordsworth's house in the Lake District and rambling walks on the Yorkshire moors.

It gave Gertrude a chill to listen to her, for she knew the source of this particular travel story. It was Madge Taylor who had vacationed two years ago in the north of England. Madge had talked about her trip at the Golden Years Club and shown everyone the postcards that she had brought back. Gertrude remembered how Connie had leaned forward to absorb every word, how she had studied every postcard, soaking it all up. Now Madge's trip to England had taken root in Connie's mind, had grown and blossomed there to become part of Connie's memories, though Connie had never been to England in her life.

Gertrude had been more fortunate than her sister. She had married, raised a family, prospered, and been generally satisfied. She supposed that was why she went along with most of Connie's stories. It would be unkind to correct her. If Connie's fantasies made her happy, why should Gertrude try to destroy them? But to start telling people that she had had a child! That was going too far.

"Ronald couldn't find a job," said Connie. She sighed deeply as she set down her cup and saucer on the very edge of the table beside her—half over the edge, in fact. Gertrude waited spellbound for it to fall, which it did, naturally, splashing milky tea onto the worn carpet.

"I'll get a cloth from the kitchen," said Gertrude, getting up.

"Thank you. That table is so tippy. Everything I set on it seems to end up on the floor."

When Gertrude had wiped up the spill, she took the cloth back to the kitchen. She took the cup and saucer away too. Neither was broken. Gertrude gave a sigh of relief; there were so few pieces left of Mother's china.

While in the kitchen, Gertrude could hear Connie's voice coming from the parlour. "Ronald had no money," Connie said.

"Ronald?" said Gertrude, coming back into the room. "Who was Ronald?"

"Ronald Wilson. You must remember him. He lived on the next street over from us."

"Yes, yes. I do remember him. Sandy-haired young fellow. Short. Very quiet. He lived with his mother. They were on Relief." Gertrude felt uncomfortable. She did not like the way this story was going.

"Ronald took me to the movies once," said Connie. "The Roxy. We saw Charlie Chaplin in *City Lights*. There was another feature, but I forget what it was. At the intermission they gave away dishes. Pretty glass dishes. I still have the bread and butter plate I got that evening."

"The pink Depression Glass plate? So that's where it came from!"

"I told Ronald that he should give it to his mother, but he said she'd be angry if she knew that he'd been to the movies. That's why he wanted me to keep it. They had no money, you know."

"I didn't know Ronald ever took you out."

"Just the once. I said that I would pay the next time because I had a job. But Ronald said no. He would never go to the movies with a girl if he couldn't pay for her ticket."

"Was Ronald sweet on you?"

"My word, yes! We used to go for walks. Then Ronald got afraid that someone would see us together and tell his mother. He didn't want to worry her. Ronald's mother was deathly afraid that he might get married and leave her. And then where would she be?"

"In the same place that she ended up anyway," said Gertrude. "After Ronald died, she went into the County Home."

"That's true," said Connie. "They never had any money."

"He was hit by a train, wasn't he?"

"Yes," said Connie, "that was how he died."

"Crossing the railroad tracks. People said he must have been trying to hop a freight train. It was tragic."

"He never knew that he had a little girl," said Connie.

Gertrude felt a cold chill down her spine. "Connie, Ronald never had a little girl. Ronald never married."

"Yes, he did. He married me." Connie smiled dreamily. "I never told anyone that before, either. We couldn't let people know … because of his mother. And if Mr. Markham had known that I was a married woman, I would have lost my job. So we didn't live together. It was very difficult for us ever to be alone." She bowed her head for a few seconds, then said, "Do you remember my blue *crepe de Chine* dress? I bought it for my wedding."

Gertrude nodded. Of course she remembered the dress. Connie had kept on wearing it for ten years. The dress, at least, had been real.

"When I suspected that I was in the family way," said Connie, "I went to a doctor. He was a special doctor for babies. One of the girls at work told me about him. His office was in a house on Napier Street."

"There weren't any doctors' offices on Napier Street."

"Oh, yes, that's where it was." Connie's cloudy eyes seemed full of light. She leaned back against the faded rose damask upholstery of her chair, thin hands clasped in her lap. "I had to go through the front parlour to another room. That was where he had all his instruments. The instruments looked terrible—so hard and shiny. One looked like tongs for picking up sugar cubes, but much bigger. There was a tiny saw with fine, sharp teeth. And knives. I started to cry and almost ran away, I was so frightened. But the doctor said not to worry. He told me that he had helped hundreds of young ladies just like me. I had to lie down on a table." Connie fell silent, and tears came to her eyes.

Gertrude waited. The clock on the mantelpiece ticked loudly. Outside, the sounds of rush hour had begun.

When Connie spoke again, her voice was firm. "It wasn't really so terrible. I was back at work after two days. Ronald never knew."

Gertrude did not say a word. In 1931 she and Connie were still sharing the same bedroom. They saw each other in every stage of dress and undress. Connie had not gotten heavy. Never. She was always thin as a rake and flat as a board. Gertrude took a deep breath. "What happened to your little girl?"

"She was adopted by well-to-do people. The doctor arranged it. They were an English couple who could give her every advantage. They took her back to England with them and sent her to the best British schools. My daughter grew up to be a lovely woman.

"I went to see her when I visited England. She is married, and she lives in the Lake District. I wish I had taken the bread and butter plate to give her, so that she would have something from her father. But I didn't think of it at the time."

Connie got up from her chair and walked across the room to the tall china cabinet where her treasures were on display. From a drawer in the lower section she took out a brass key. Her hands shook so much she could scarcely get the key into the keyhole. Gertrude watched as Connie fumbled to unlock the glass-fronted door.

"Connie, may I help you? Do you want me to get out the plate for you?"

"I can manage," said Connie. But as she picked up the plate, it slipped from her hand, struck the edge of the china cabinet as it fell, and shattered on the parquet floor. Connie stood motionless, staring at the broken glass that lay in a hundred shards and slivers at her feet.

Gertrude went to Connie, took her hand and led her back to her chair. Connie sat down, leaned against the cushions and looked up at Gertrude. "I shouldn't have tried to take out the plate," she said. "It was safe in the cabinet so long as I left it there. But I wanted to share it with you." Connie's eyes filled with tears.

"It was very fragile," said Gertrude gently. She stood looking down at Connie, whose cheeks were wet with tears. "Let me sweep it up. I don't want you to get hurt from handling pieces of broken glass."

On her way to get a dustpan and brush from the kitchen, Gertrude passed Connie's chair and paused for a moment to pat Connie's shoulder. Beneath the thin fabric of her dress, there seemed to be nothing but bone. Gertrude swept up the glass.

"There!" she said. "I'll dump this in the trash can and make us a fresh pot of tea." The fragments of pink glass in the dustpan gleamed in the light of the table lamp by Connie's chair. Connie turned her face away. "Now, Connie," said Gertrude, "You must put it out of your mind. There's no great loss." She was about to say that it was a cheap plate, but stopped herself in time.

Catnappers

"Throw it!" said Jane.

Cindy was holding the Coca-Cola bottle by the neck, waggling it back and forth.

"For Chrissake, don't just stand there."

Cindy raised her arm and hurled the bottle. It seemed to fly through the air in slow motion, turning a half somersault so that the heel of the bottle struck the window. One moment there was a smooth pane of glass gleaming in the light of the street lamp. And the next there was a star with a black hole at the centre and rays all around. The Coke bottle disappeared into the black hole.

"Good throw!" said Jane, grabbing Cindy's arm. "Now let's get out of here!"

The two girls raced up Mrs. Winfield's driveway, across

her backyard, and through the gate into the alley. They squatted in a dark corner by an old garage, listening to Mrs. Winfield open her back door. Her walker made a thumping sound as she came out onto the porch.

The girls looked at each other. Cindy giggled.

"Ssh!" Jane warned.

After a few more thumps the door shut. Mrs. Winfield had gone back inside.

"We should go home now." Cindy stood up.

"No," said Jane, pulling Cindy back down beside her. Her heart pounded with excitement. "Give her a minute to find the note in the Coke bottle. I want to hear what happens after she reads it."

Using words and letters cut from weekend flyers and a paperback copy of *The Call of the Wild*, they had made a ransom note telling Mrs. Winfield what she had to do:

Leave one hundred dollars in five-dollar bills in the Player's cigarette box that is stuck in your hedge. Or we kill your cat. Don't tell anyone or you'll never see your cat again. You have till Saturday, May 6.

"I'm going home," said Cindy. "I don't want to be here when she calls the cops."

"She won't call the cops. She wouldn't dare."

The back door opened again. Mrs. Winfield thumped across the porch.

"Ssh!" Jane whispered. "She's come back out."

Mrs. Winfield stood on her back porch and called, "Panther! Panther! Here, kitty kitty!" She stood out there for at least five minutes calling "Panther!" and "Kitty Kitty!" The girls could hear her start to cry.

"It's going to work," Jane whispered. "She'll pay."

Cindy and Jane had milk and cookies when they got home. Then they went up to their bedroom to do their homework. They had always shared a room. It seemed natural that they should, being twins. Their younger brother Rocky had a room to himself. They were eleven years old; he was only six.

After doing their homework, the girls went to bed. Jane was in the upper bunk. She was afraid that Cindy might fall asleep, so she threw things at her from time to time: her slippers, an eraser, pencils—nothing that would make a noise. They lay there listening to the sound of the television downstairs, and then to Mom and Dad getting ready for bed. When they could hear Dad snoring, they got up and dressed quietly. The clock on their dresser read 12:15.

The houses were close together in the east end of the city. Most had been built about eighty years ago, in pairs, with about one metre between two houses, then a shared driveway, then another pair of houses, then another driveway, and so on. Every block had a lane, called the back alley, running through the middle. There were fences, sheds and garages all along the lane. Some of the sheds were in use, but many were rundown, left to rot away.

Cindy and Jane liked to poke around in the old sheds. Sometimes they found neat things. In an old wooden shed two blocks north of the house where they lived, they had found a dog crate. That was what gave them the idea for the kidnapping. They called it catnapping, because it sounded funny. Mom, who had insomnia if she didn't take her sleeping pills, was always sneaking catnaps during the day. The shed was perfect too, because it had no windows—just a door that sagged on its hinges. It looked like nobody had used it for years.

Jane smelled cat pee as soon as she opened the shed door. She went in first, flicking on her flashlight as soon as Cindy had closed the door. In the beam of light, Panther's eyes were golden globes. When Cindy released the catch on the crate, Panther stepped out slowly, his motions deliberate.

"Here, kitty," Cindy said, stroking his back. He purred and kept pushing his head against her leg while she put kibble into one dish and water into the other. Jane cleaned his litter box.

Panther struggled when Jane shoved him back into the crate. His claws raked her arm.

"Damn cat!" she said.

"Maybe we should let him go," said Cindy.

"Don't be an idiot. We can't let him go until Mrs. Winfield hands over the ransom."

In the morning the cat scratch on Jane's arm was red and sore. She had no sooner sat down for breakfast when Rocky knocked over his glass. Milk flowed across the table and dribbled over the edge. Some of it got on Jane's skirt.

"Asshole!" she said.

Mom glared. "Watch your language!"

Jane glared right back, pretending that her eyes were a double-barrelled ray gun shooting deadly beams into Mom's eyes. In a moment Mom's eyes would explode, and eyeball jelly would fly all over the table.

"Fuck off!" Jane said triumphantly.

Mom looked at Dad, who was reading his newspaper and probably hadn't heard a thing. "Are you going to let her get away with that?" she demanded, punching the back of his newspaper to make sure he paid attention.

Dad lowered his newspaper. "Our local arsonist has been busy again," he said. "Last night he torched a garage on Holton Avenue. The heat melted the vinyl siding on the house next door. Lucky the house didn't burn." He folded the newspaper and stood up. "That's the third fire this month. The police think he uses the back alleys to move about."

Now Mom was mad at Dad too. "Didn't you hear what I said?"

"About Jane swearing? She does it to get attention. Ignore it, and she'll stop."

Jane gave Mom her sweetest smile.

Jane and Cindy passed Mrs. Winfield's house on their way to school. A piece of cardboard had been taped over the broken window. The cigarette box was still in the hedge, placed exactly as they had left it. "I guess she hasn't put the money in it yet," said Cindy.

"She's got to go to the bank first. Not likely she has a hundred dollars in five-dollar bills in her purse."

"I guess not."

"We'll give her until Saturday, like we said, before we go on to the next stage. That's just two more days."

The back alley was empty that afternoon. For a change, there weren't any little kids hanging around having a smoke. Cindy and Jane sneaked into the shed without being seen. Panther, crouched in his crate, shot out like a missile as soon as Cindy released the catch. No pats and purrs this time. He raced from one side of the shed to the other, bumping against walls and hurling himself at the door. His meowing was barely a hoarse croak.

"Panther's got laryngitis," Cindy said.

"That's good," said Jane. "If people can't hear him, they aren't going to get curious and start snooping round."

Panther dug in his claws when Cindy tried to return him to the crate. He writhed and squirmed in his frenzy to escape. It took both of them to shove him back inside.

"Maybe we ought to snitch one of Mom's sleeping pills," said Cindy as she latched the crate door. "We could give him bits of sleeping pill in his food. That would quiet him down."

Jane stood guard in the front hall while Cindy went upstairs to look for the sleeping pills. Mom was out in the garden murdering slugs, but she might come in anytime.

Cindy's footsteps moved from the tile floor of the bathroom to the carpeting of Mom and Dad's bedroom. Jane sat perfectly still on the bottom step of the staircase. She heard drawers open and close. "For Chrissake, hurry up," she muttered.

Cindy came down the stairs with one tiny pill in her hand. She showed it to Jane. "The bottle said sodium seconal. Does that sound right?"

"I guess so. What took you so long?"

"The sleeping pills weren't in the medicine cabinet. Mom had them in her bedside table along with her birth control pills."

Jane snickered. "We should give Panther a birth control pill. Just to see what happens."

"That's a dumb idea," said Cindy. "Panther's a boy."

A couple of little kids were smoking in the back alley after school, so it was not safe to visit the shed. "Shit," Jane said. "We'll have to come back after supper."

"But Panther's been all alone since yesterday."

"He can survive for another two hours."

Mom was waiting for them. "Where have you two been? I told you to come straight home after school to clean your room. It looks like a pigpen."

"All right, all right," said Jane. "You don't have to make such a big deal out of it."

"That's enough," Mom said, thrusting a garbage can into Jane's hand. "You're both grounded until it's cleaned up."

"Ah, fuck," Jane said as she headed up the stairs carrying a garbage bag.

"Yeah," Cindy agreed. "But our room is a mess."

The girls tossed the empty soft drink cans and candy wrappers into the garbage bag. Socks and underwear, picked up from the floor, went into the laundry hamper. Cindy found a bowl of something scummy hiding on the windowsill behind a drape.

"What the fuck is this?" she asked.

"Let me see," Jane said. "Oh yeah, that's the strawberry ice cream I brought up here last week."

Mom came up to check on the girls every half hour. She even made them dust and vacuum. It was nine o'clock before they had the room clean to Mom's satisfaction. They weren't allowed to go out that late, so they made popcorn and watched TV.

They went to bed still wearing their clothes. Cindy was feeling sorry for Panther. "He hasn't seen anybody since after school yesterday," she said. "He must be frightened."

"He'll be fine for a couple more hours," said Jane. "Tonight we can give him some of that tinned cat food. We'll put Mom's sleeping pill in it. That should keep him dozy until tomorrow, when Mrs. Winfield pays the ransom."

"Let's just give him half," said Cindy.

Mom and Dad went to bed at the usual time, but they didn't go right to sleep. Sounds of laughter came from their bedroom, then the squeaking of springs. Jane pulled her pillow over her head so she wouldn't have to listen. Jane knew what was going on; she thought it was absolutely disgusting.

When she pushed the pillow off her head, she heard nothing. Dad wasn't snoring, and there was no sound from the lower bunk.

"Cindy!"

No answer.

"Cindy, are you asleep?"

Still no answer. Jane scrambled down the ladder. There was Cindy, fast asleep with her arms around her teddy bear. Jane shook Cindy roughly by the shoulder. "Wake up!" she hissed. Cindy slumbered on. Jane had to pull the blankets completely off her to get any response.

"What?" Cindy moaned.

"Ssh! We've got to take care of the cat."

Jane picked up her shoes and tiptoed to the door. Cindy stumbled out of bed and knocked over her desk chair on her way across the room. Jane held her breath. But the noise did not wake Mom or Dad. As for Rocky, he would sleep through a tornado.

They let themselves out the side door and hurried up the driveway, past the garage, and through their back gate into the lane. It was a gusty night. Overhead, tree branches creaked as they rubbed together. From a couple of blocks away the girls heard the honking bellow of a fire truck's horn and the siren of a police car going east on Main Street. Jane and Cindy kept in the shadows as they headed down the back alley. Cindy took Jane's hand.

When they got to the shed, Panther did not greet them. He raised his head only when the flashlight shone upon him. All they could see of the black cat lying on the floor of the crate were the twin golden lamps of his eyes. He did not stand up. "Panther must be sick," Cindy whispered. She lifted him out of the crate and cuddled him in her arms.

The food dish and water bowl were empty. The stench of cat excrement fouled the air. Jane cleaned the kitty litter box first, because the mess was so gross. Then she filled the water bowl and spooned cat food into Panther's dish. She put the whole sleeping pill into the cat food so that Panther would be sure to stay asleep.

He lapped up the bowlful of water and ate every bit of the food. After Panther had drunk and eaten, the only thing he wanted to do was lie on Cindy's lap and purr. The girls did not rush away. Panther was asleep when they put him back in the crate.

As soon as they left the shed, they saw a bright glow in the eastern sky. It didn't look like sunrise. It was too pink, and it was all in one spot. "Fire!" Jane said.

"Remember," said Cindy, "we heard the fire engine and the cop car going that way."

"The arsonist!" Jane shivered. Somewhere in the back alleys of the east end there was a prowling criminal. They looked over their shoulders with every step as they hurried home.

The morning newspaper contained no report of a fire. "It must have happened too late to meet the paper's deadline," Jane said.

After breakfast Cindy and Jane strolled by Mrs. Winfield's house. The cigarette package was gone, but so were all the other bits of litter that had accumulated over the winter months. There was no remaining trace of discarded tissues, paper coffee cups, or water-stained flyers. Mrs. Winfield's borders, flower beds and lawn looked freshly raked.

"Damn," said Jane. "Now we don't know whether Mrs. Winfield took the cigarette box into the house to put the money into it, or whether the garden clean-up guy threw it out with the other garbage."

"Maybe she'd already put the money into the Player's box and the clean-up guy found it. I bet he wouldn't tell anybody if he found a hundred dollars in some old lady's hedge."

"I bet he threw out the cigarette box without looking inside," said Jane.

The girls walked on, heads together, considering the possibilities. Today was Saturday, May 6, the deadline. Jane said it didn't matter whether somebody else got the hundred bucks or not. If Mrs. Winfield had been dumb enough to put out the money when the clean-up guy was coming, that was her own fault. Jane and Cindy must go on to stage two of their plan.

"I don't want to hurt Panther," said Cindy.

"We won't hurt him. It isn't as if we were going cut off his tail or one of his ears. Just his whiskers. It won't be any different from getting your hair cut, or Dad shaving. We'll just trim his whiskers, put them in an envelope, and shove it through Mrs. Winfield's mail slot. She'll know whose whiskers they are."

When Cindy and Jane got back home, they turned on the television to watch the noon news. Now there was a report on the fire. A vacant store had been torched. The arsonist had used gasoline-soaked rags shoved against the back door. The Chief of Police made a statement: "We are asking the public to be vigilant. We must apprehend the perpetrator before there is loss of life."

All day long people were outside working in their back-yards. Cindy and Jane had no opportunity to visit the shed. In the evening Mom and Dad took Rocky and the girls to a movie. Once again it was past midnight when Cindy and Jane left their house.

Cindy had Mom's manicure scissors in her jeans' pocket. Jane had the envelope into which they would put the whiskers, to be dropped through Mrs. Winfield's letter slot on the girls' way home. They scurried along the lane like a pair of mice, keeping close to the fences.

They were halfway down the lane when they saw the flame shoot up from the shed. It rose with a whooshing sound and flared like a pillar of fire higher than the shed roof. By its light they saw someone on a bicycle come straight toward them. The bike was old, with no lights. The rider was hunched over the handlebars. As it passed by, Jane saw a man's face under the long visor of a baseball cap. Cindy and Jane pressed their bodies against the back fence. Jane did not breathe until the bicycle reached the street at the end of the lane, turned right, and was gone.

Cindy was already racing towards the shed as if she didn't care whether anybody saw her or not. Jane caught up just as Cindy reached the shed door. All Jane could hear was the roar of the flames. Cindy had her hand on the latch when Jane grabbed her arm and pulled her away.

"Let me go!" Cindy screamed. "I've got to save Panther."

"No!" Jane shouted. "It's too late."

In seconds flames engulfed the shed. Tears rolled down Cindy's cheeks. Jane gulped hard so that she wouldn't start crying too. "Panther had the whole sleeping pill," Jane said. "He didn't feel a thing."

There was a loud bang from inside the shed. Jane wanted to run, but her feet would not move. They heard shouts from a house across the lane. The shed was an inferno.

The girls were still standing in the lane when the fire truck and the police arrived. They did not talk in the police car on their way to the station. Each sat huddled on her own side of the back seat. Jane noticed that there were no door or window handles. We've been arrested, she thought. We're in big trouble now.

At the police station Cindy cried. The policeman who talked to them thought she was just crying because she got caught. Jane told the police about the man on the bike, but they didn't believe her.

"If you girls didn't start the fire, what were you doing in the lane at one in the morning?"

"I don't know," Cindy sniffled.

"I don't know," said Jane.

"Then there's two of you who don't know what you were doing in the lane when the fire started. Isn't that a bit strange?"

"Maybe," said Jane.

A policewoman searched the girls. All she found on them were a pair of manicure scissors and an empty envelope. She said that she couldn't figure it out.

The police phoned Mom and Dad. When Dad arrived, he looked very tired. There were bags like little grey pouches under his eyes. He talked with the police for a long time. Then the police let him take the girls home. When they got into the car, Dad said, "You might have been killed." Cindy cried all the way home.

Dad marched the two girls ahead of him into the house.

Mom was sitting at the kitchen table, wearing her dressing gown and drinking a cup of tea. She looked as if she was in shock.

"You sneaked out in the middle of the night." Mom's voice was shaking. "The police picked you up watching a fire in the back alley. You girls have some explaining to do." Mom waited. No answer.

Mom stared at Jane, and Jane met her stare, eye to eye. "I woke up in the middle of the night," Jane said. "I thought I heard something strange, so I looked out the window. There was this man riding a bicycle with no lights on. I thought it was probably the arsonist, so I woke Cindy up and made her go out with me to catch him."

Mom and Dad looked as if they didn't believe her, but didn't disbelieve her either.

"We'll deal with this tomorrow," Dad said. "Go to bed."

By the time they had changed into their pyjamas, Cindy had stopped crying. "That was pretty smart—what you said."

"Yeah," Jane said as she climbed the ladder to her bunk, "So long as we stick to that story, nobody ever needs to know the rest."

Cindy and Jane were grounded all the next day. They studied for a history test. Mom made them do some vacuuming. Watching television was forbidden. The girls did not talk to each other about Panther or the fire.

On Monday morning they passed Mrs. Winfield's house on the way to school. There was a Player's box stuck in the hedge in the exact spot where they had placed it four days earlier. It looked full, as if there might be money stuffed inside. Cindy saw it and looked away. Jane knelt to tie her shoelaces. When she stood up, the box was gone.

Josie's Custom Catering

"Don't I know you?" drawls the woman in the red dress. She has a languid voice, but her eyes are sharp.

"I don't think so."

"Kingston. Maybe ten years ago?"

"I've never been to Kingston." I smile apologetically, as if sorry to disappoint her.

"Oh, well," she shrugs. "I must be wrong."

"Maybe I have a double." I keep smiling as I carry my platter of hors d'oeuvres to the next circle of talking faces. Has anyone noticed that the tray is shaking in my hands?

As soon as my platter is half empty, I take it into the kitchen. This is routine. Offering canapés from a half-empty platter is nearly as tacky as serving leftovers. In the catering business, presentation is everything.

In the kitchen, I take a deep breath and straighten my smile. Then back to the fray with a fresh platter to work the other end of the room. If I'm lucky, the woman in the red dress has already forgotten about the server with the familiar face.

I'm not lucky. I see her standing beside a woman gowned in black, both of them peering around the room, their bejewelled necks stretched like a pair of cranes trying to see over people's heads.

Red Dress spots me, points me out to Black Gown. The women lean their heads toward each other, whisper behind their fingers. Black Gown frowns, shakes her head. That's good. Maybe Red Dress will lose interest.

I know where they've seen my face before. Ten years ago I was front-page news. Anyone who read newspapers or watched TV knew what I looked like. But I'm older now, twenty pounds heavier and no longer blond. Nine people out of ten wouldn't recognize me today. Nine out of ten don't remember *Josie's Custom Catering*.

I was Josie, Kingston's most exclusive caterer for elegant parties with fifty to two hundred guests. Wives hired me for my Cordon Bleu presentation. Husbands liked me, and it wasn't my hot canapés that turned them on. They hovered in the background, hopping to attention whenever there was a door to open, a heavy carton to lift. They looked at me—all Paris style with my pale blond hair in a chignon, long legs, skinny high heels—then they looked at their wives.

I was twenty-eight years old, a triple S woman—smart, stylish, successful—and I didn't care who knew it.

The girls I hired were trim and short. They wore chic little caps and frilly aprons. No one mistook them for guests.

Now I'm the one wearing the cap and apron. Now my name is Marlene.

Josie's Custom Catering had business cards, but I never pressed people to take them. Nor did I advertise. It was better to make clients search for me. And I wouldn't cater a private event for just anyone. A big house with a good address wasn't enough. I needed to know what car my client drove, where she summered, and—this was critical—where her money came from. Due diligence, they call it.

Love ruined me. His name was Roger Bellamy. Since the trial, everyone knows that name. It was in the papers every day. So was mine.

Roger was worth about ten million. Old money had given him a start, but he had tripled it in twenty years. He was forty-five when I met him, the age when a man may be tempted to trade in his original wife for a newer model.

And he did have a wife. Rosalind Bellamy was a small pointy woman: pointy nose, pointy chin, and pointy breasts. Even her dyed black hair in its pixie cut came to points. She had a sly face with a wide mouth that displayed slightly prominent teeth. Her restless brown eyes flashed disdain at everything inferior to herself, which she thought included me. Twenty years earlier she may have been described as

perky. Now she alternated between a weasel and a bitch. I
had heard that she drank, but that was just a rumour.

Asking discreetly, I learned that Roger and Rosalind had
two almost-grown children, who were away at university.

Roger spent little time at home. He served on boards—
high profile ones, like the hospital and the symphony, which
had gala fundraisers. That was where *Josie's Custom Catering*
came in, my girls in their chic uniforms passing the hors
d'oeuvres and keeping the wineglasses filled.

A symphony fundraiser at Bellevue House brought us
together. He was convener, so even though it was two in the
morning, he had to wait around until my girls had cleaned
up.

"Where are you from?" he asked me. His tone was casual,
making polite conversation.

"Windsor." I was busy counting tablecloths, making sure
I left with the same number I had brought. I always checked.
Not just tablecloths, but wineglasses, platters, and serving
dishes. Experience had taught me to count everything
before leaving the premises. That's the only way to prevent
shrinkage.

"What brought you to Kingston?" He sat on a chair at
one of the empty tables, his eyes following me as I crammed
the tablecloths into garbage bags.

"Opportunity."

"Why Kingston?"

"Kingston needed me. I saw a niche waiting for me to
fill."

"You've done well, considering you're still very young."

"I started young." I fastened the top of the garbage bag with a twist-tie. "Custom catering was the only thing I ever wanted to do. After high school, I spent two years working for a caterer while I saved up for the Cordon Bleu school in Paris."

"But what attracted you to the catering business? Family connections?"

That made me laugh. "My mother is a cellist who's never quite made it. My father is a sculptor who worked twenty years to get his first commission."

"You make me even more curious."

"Well, then, I'll tell you." I gave him a quick smile as I pulled up a chair and sat down beside him, close enough to give him a whiff of my scent—two drops of Shiseido's *Eau de Zen* behind my ears. "I chose catering because I loved good food." He shifted in his seat, draping his arm across the back of my chair. I pretended not to notice. "After a recital or an opening, my parents brought home leftovers. Canapés. Half a chocolate cheesecake. Except for those, I grew up on fried bologna and peanut butter sandwiches."

As I huddled beside him, not wanting the girls to hear, I felt his arm touch my back. This was too fast. I stood up.

"All finished," one of the girls called out. "Shall we load the van?"

Standing at the door, I flipped the top of every carton as they carried it outside. You have to be careful or staff will rob you blind.

While the girls loaded my van, I called taxis to send them home.

Roger waited until the last taxi had left, then walked me to my van. He stood closer than necessary as he opened the door.

"Are you married?" he asked.

"No."

"Boyfriend?"

"No."

"That's surprising." I saw the glint of interest in his eyes, the approval.

I laughed. "Who'd want to date a girl who works six nights a week?"

"I would," he said, bending his head toward me. "What about the seventh night?"

"Aren't you married?" Kingston is a small city. With my business to protect, I had to play the line, not cross it.

We couldn't date. Yet Roger Bellamy had everything I was looking for in a husband: social position, plenty of money, and five generations of ancestors buried in Cataraqui Cemetery. As a bonus, he was attractive. Any man would be attractive in the kind of suits he wore, but Roger would have been good-looking in rags. He was tall, lean, and walked with a slight stoop that was oddly elegant. His eyes were blue. The skin at the outer corners of his eyes crinkled slightly when he smiled. I found that sexy. His money was sexy too.

We kept bumping into each other after that evening. The library. Malls. Parking lots. We both seemed to have antennae waving in the air, searching.

At first, our meetings were accidental, but later deliberate, at least on my part. I started going to symphony concerts on Sunday afternoons. He was usually there. So was Rosalind. I chatted with them at intermissions. She thought she knew all about music. If Roger had an opinion she didn't share, her voice went higher and higher, louder and louder. You'd think that Mozart, Beethoven and Richard Strauss had personally explained to her exactly how their music should be played. I smiled politely and kept my opinions to myself.

It was only a matter of time before Rosalind needed my professional services. She had in mind a smaller affair than I usually catered, a gathering in her home. About forty people—women she had gone to school with. Naturally, Roger wouldn't be there.

I took the booking because I wanted to be in the house where he lived, walk over carpets that he walked over, touch plates that he ate from, drink from a glass that he had held in his hand.

When the maid let me into the Bellamy house, the same hushed feeling came over me that I get when I enter a cathedral, not just because it's beautiful, but because of its mystical ambience.

In this case, the mystical ambience lasted ten seconds. A crash shattered it, followed by a scream. The maid tore into the kitchen with me at her heels. And there was Rosalind, leaning against the counter as she stared at the wreckage of three dozen wineglasses scattered all over the floor.

"Don't worry!" I said calmly. "Your guests won't arrive for another two hours. There's plenty of time to clean this up and get more glasses." Rosalind's eyes were blurry. I figured that she had already sampled too much wine.

I was wrong about that. After I had chased Rosalind out of the kitchen—it's my cardinal rule never to let the lady of the house get in my way—I began to find vodka bottles.

Normally I'm too professional to snoop. But this time the temptation was irresistible. I found bottles in the vegetable crisper, in the freezer, and under the kitchen sink. There was one behind the olive oil in the cupboard over the stove. Some bottles were full, some half empty. I should have felt sorry for Rosalind, but I didn't. Gleeful was more like it.

The broom cupboard had its vodka bottle too, but what caught my eye was the dusty bottle right beside it on the shelf. It was round-shouldered and glass stoppered, with a skull on the label. Above the skull were the words Carbon Tetrachloride, and under it in big letters: POISON. The bottle was half full of a clear liquid, as clear as vodka.

Rosalind's party was a success. She was too busy chatting with her old school pals to get any tipsier than she started out. The canapés were perfect.

Roger arrived home as I was getting into the van. He parked his Jaguar and came over to talk to me. When I opened the window, he leaned in toward me. His face was so close that I felt the warmth of his breath and smelled his Hermes cologne. He was near enough to kiss.

"How did it go?" he asked.

"Just fine." He had me off balance. I started babbling all sorts of things—like the kinds of cheese on the cheese tray and how I shouldn't have made so many crab pasties. The atmosphere felt charged, the way it does before a thunderstorm. I could hardly tell which words were in my head and which I was saying out loud. But I definitely did tell him about the poison.

"Do you know there's half a bottle of carbon tetrachloride on your broom closet shelf?"

"I'm not surprised. My grandmother's maid used to use it for spot removal, and it's probably been sitting there ever since. Last year I found DDT in the garage. These old properties stay in the same family for a century and never get cleared out."

"Maybe you should have a good housecleaning."

"Maybe I should. Someday I'll get around to it."

Why did I tell him about the carbon tetrachloride? I suppose that I wanted him to find Rosalind's vodka. But mostly my mouth was making noise.

A month went by before I saw Roger again. It was my busiest time of year—the Christmas season. I was doing a last-minute check of the buffet table before the Art Gallery's holiday party, admiring a salmon mousse which I had moulded in the shape of a fish—perfect to its scales and the bones in its fins—when Roger stepped up beside me.

For a minute he didn't say anything. We stood side by side staring at the fish. When his sleeve brushed my arm, I felt a tingling sensation deep inside. Then he spoke: "Do you like opera?"

"It depends on the opera."

"They're doing *The Marriage of Figaro* in Mississauga."

"Mississauga?" Not Toronto, not Montreal, but Mississauga—where nobody goes. Afterward there would be a motel. Lips meeting. Hands caressing. Bodies joining. Suddenly I felt so lightheaded I could scarcely draw in breath.

"When?"

"Friday, January 20."

"I'll check my calendar."

Rosalind came up to us then. She was wearing a low-cut cocktail dress and triple pearls at her throat—an outfit apparently chosen to emphasize the prominence of her collarbones. She smiled coldly and led Roger away, leaving me breathless beside the salmon mousse.

In the motel, I called him Alma Viva while he undid the buttons of my blouse. "*Droît du Seigneur*," he said. Now I realize that he meant it. Then I didn't know.

From that day on, the edges of my life began to crumble. Roger was in my space, and there was hardly room for anything but him. Lies and lust. I moved in a fog of love, everything a blur.

He took a compass and made two concentric circles upon a map, with Kingston at the centre. Every place within the inner circle was too close to home. Every place beyond the outer circle was too far to drive. Belleville, Brockville, Smith Falls, Alexandria Bay. That was our Tropic of Capricorn, our zone of love.

By April it was clear that people knew. One client dropped me, then another. Casual acquaintances averted their eyes.

I had to mobilize my brain, love-addled though it was.

I broke the news while we lay on rumpled sheets in the Shady Rest Motel on Highway 2 outside Joyceville. "We can't keep this up," I told Roger. "I can't be screwing my clients' husbands. It's bad for business."

"I don't want to lose you," he said, putting his hand between my legs.

"Well, what's the alternative?"

This was his chance. He just looked depressed. Darkness seemed to creep from the corners of the room.

"We'd better take a time out," he said. "When tongues stop wagging, we'll get back together. But be more careful."

What was that? Not 'goodbye forever,' but not 'happily ever after' either. I dusted off my pride.

"Definitely, we'll have to be more discreet," I said. We made love again. Roger had missed his cue.

It took all summer for me to find my missing pieces and put myself together again. By September the sound of his name no longer caused my heart to thud. Finally I could see Roger at social functions without my knees turning to water. I practised smiling coolly. I got him out of my space. Business picked up. My clients looked relieved, even apologetic, as if ashamed for having believed false rumours. I was not a *femme fatale* after all. Their husbands were safe.

Then Roger phoned me. "I need you. I can't live without you." At his words I felt a sweet shudder deep inside. "Rosalind is in Vancouver visiting her sister. The maid doesn't come in on weekends. We'll have the house to ourselves."

And the bed, I thought. The matrimonial bed. I squeezed my eyes shut and conjured up a vision of how it would be. I would lie between silken sheets, flawless as a polished pearl. In the morning I would awake with Roger beside me, his head close to mine on the pillow. He would see that this was where I belonged.

"Too risky," I said, taking a deep breath. "Someone might see me going in or leaving. People would start talking again, and next time the gossip wouldn't stop."

"I'll pick you up in my car. You can hunch down so nobody sees you. We can drive straight into the garage and leave the same way."

Thank God for attached garages!

"Well, if we're careful." I hesitated long enough to make him think I had trouble making up my mind. "How does this sound? Saturday evening, nine o'clock, I'll be parked at the far end of the VIA Station lot on Counter Street. Meet me there. I can stay with you until Sunday noon. I'll bring stuff to cook. We'll have brunch."

As I hung up the phone, I congratulated myself on my quick thinking. After great sex, a great brunch. I would cook something exquisite. I saw myself standing at the stove in Roger's kitchen. An omelette? Eggs Benedict? Roger, sitting across the table from me, would see how well I blended with the decor. Over Cordon Bleu he would realize how happy we would be as husband and wife in the Bellamy family home.

The bedroom had a high ceiling, with tall, valanced windows. The walls were papered with dark, flocked wallpaper that made me think of red *fleurs-de-lys* stacked in columns. I would get rid of it. Paint would be less oppressive. Maybe a mushroom shade, textured. But I'd have to give the colour some thought.

From the moment I entered the bedroom, I had the feeling that someone else was there besides Roger and me. Rosalind? No. Someone from another generation. Roger's mother? His grandmother? Bellamy wives have walked over these creaking floors for a century. Someday I would be able to ask Roger about these women.

I lay beside Roger imagining scenarios. Although the velvet drapes were closed, I could see that it was no longer dark outside. I could not sleep, although we had spent half the night making love. Now he lay on his back, snoring quietly, his hand on my thigh as if he were holding me in place. I heard the birds wake up, chirping.

Rising on one elbow, I looked down at Roger's face, at the slashes of grey in his sideburns and the crow's feet at his eyes. At the sight of him sleeping, I felt a stab of something poignant. Love? Not exactly. But close enough. If I married Roger, I'd have it all.

Carefully I removed his hand from my thigh and climbed out of bed. A quick wash. There was no bidet in the bathroom. Just as well. That was one thing I would not want to share with Rosalind.

When I crawled back under the covers, we made love again. Sex with Roger was always great. So great that both of us could have done without the brunch and stayed in bed for another round. We probably would have, if Roger hadn't said, "Would you marry me if I were free?"

Another stab of feeling, but this time it was anger. "You can ask that question when you are free."

"I would," he said. "Believe me, I would."

I noticed the "would." Josie, I said to myself, you're wasting your time. He's married, and he intends to stay married. I felt cheated, as I would with a customer who tasted all my samples but didn't place an order. No way I could settle for less than marriage. I wasn't going to throw away five years of hard work for a chance to crawl between the sheets with somebody else's husband a couple of times a month.

For about five minutes neither of us said anything. I sat up and was about to swing my legs over the side of the bed, when Roger grabbed my shoulders and pulled me back down.

"Josie," he said reproachfully, "don't be angry. Sneaking around isn't my style any more that it's yours. I wish I could sleep with you every night. I wish I could spend the rest of my life with you. I would marry you if I were free."

"You've already said that." My muscles tensed. I wasn't going to plead.

"There's nothing more I can say. I can't leave Rosalind. She's too fragile. She'd fall apart, and several people I love very much would never forgive me. For me to get a divorce would be more complicated than you can imagine."

I didn't say anything. Lots of people who divorce and remarry appear to survive the complications. To push Roger would achieve nothing.

"It would be different if she left me," he said. "But she won't. There's no magic wand to make her disappear."

Disappear. Like intergalactic matter into a black hole. I visualized a swirling tunnel of darkness with Rosalind twisting and turning as it sucked her in. In her wake, all the complications would disappear too. It would be so simple. And the way to make it happen came to me like a revelation.

I turned my head toward the clock on the bedside table. Eleven thirty. Roger didn't see me smile as I got up.

This time he didn't try to stop me, but lay back against the pillows, watching me walk naked around the room. Yesterday's *Globe and Mail*, still folded, lay on a chair. I handed it to him, leaned over him and kissed him.

"I'm going to shower and dress," I said. "Then I'll prepare brunch."

"Need any help?"

"No. I can handle everything."

I sliced Portobello mushrooms while listening for Roger to turn on the shower. He seemed to be taking a long time, probably reading the newspaper first. I heated olive oil, tossed in the mushrooms, and added a splash of brandy.

Upstairs the shower started. Now I could do it. The bottle of carbon tetrachloride had not been removed from the broom closet shelf, but a new, not quite full bottle of vodka stood beside it. I got out both. Holding them to the light, I couldn't tell the one liquid from the other.

I opened the vodka first, carefully observing the level before pouring one inch of vodka down the sink. Then I pulled out the stopper from the bottle of carbon tetrachloride. I noted the exact level of the liquid in that bottle too.

It was hard to keep my hand steady as I poured. Precisely one inch; I didn't spill a drop. Then I poured tap water into the carbon tetrachloride bottle up to the original level.

After wiping it to remove fingerprints, I put both bottles back on the broom closet shelf. The carbon tetrachloride bottle no longer looked dusty. Would anyone notice? As soon as I became Mrs. Roger Bellamy, a major housecleaning would take place.

Laughter built in my chest as I thought about Rosalind lifting the vodka bottle to her lips. Funny cocktail. Not quite a martini. I could hardly stop myself from laughing out loud.

Upstairs a toilet flushed. Roger would soon be down. It was time to put the mushrooms back on the burner and turn up the heat.

How often did Rosalind visit each of her bottles? Was it random? Or had she a pattern? How long would it be before the vodka bottle in the broom closet had its turn?

Rosalind returned from Vancouver one week after my night in the Bellamy home.

Outwardly, life went on as usual. Business was good, and my days went well. Nights were different. Either I couldn't get to sleep or, if I did, I would awaken about four in the morning, shaking and sweating. What if Roger, not Rosalind, drank the poisoned vodka? Or even the maid? Of course that wouldn't happen. But what if it did?

Every morning I looked at the death notices in the news-paper, dreading and hoping at the same time. Roger didn't call me, nor did I expect him to. For the next two weeks I felt as if I were holding my breath, holding it so long that my lungs were about to burst, waiting for the moment when I could exhale.

Then it happened. The death notice appeared on October 3. "Bellamy, Rosalind. Suddenly, at home ... Beloved wife of Roger Bellamy. Loving mother of Julia and James ..."

The tough part was over.

I skipped the funeral. This was the time to lie low, wait for Roger to make the next move. Work kept me busy. Once in a while I felt a wild urge to turn down a client. I imagined saying to one of the snootier matrons: "So sorry I can't do your daughter's wedding reception, but I expect to be on my honeymoon at that time."

Roger had found Rosalind's body lying on the kitchen floor, the vodka bottle open on the counter. Her glass had slipped from her hand. I learned those details and many others from my clients. "They say that her heart simply stopped," said one lady in a hushed tone. "Rosalind had a drinking problem, you know."

"Terribly sad," I murmured. "Mr. Bellamy must be devas-tated."

I waited by the phone. My heart leapt every time it rang, but it was never Roger on the line. A month went by, then another, and another. Roger was right to be cautious, I persuaded myself. He had his own reputation as well as mine to protect. Patience was necessary, but it was hard. Roger would call soon. I knew he would.

I picked up pamphlets from a travel agency to read while I sat by the phone. The Côte d'Azur looked lovely. Roger would admire my fluency in French.

I was dreaming about azure seas when my doorbell rang. My heart jumped. Roger! At last! I dashed into the bathroom to check my hair and makeup in the mirror. The doorbell rang again.

The smile on my face didn't last long. When I opened the door, two police officers stood on the stoop.

The investigation was discreet, for who would wish to drag the respected name of Bellamy through the mud? Until arrests were made, the media had been kept in the dark.

Roger was charged with first-degree murder: intentionally causing the death of a human being. The charge against me was conspiracy to commit murder. We had separate trials. They tried Roger first. He pleaded innocent.

Free on bail, I sat in the public gallery of Frontenac County Court House every day of his trial. He saw me there, but the only time our eyes met, he looked away.

According to the Crown, Roger had possessed motive, means, and opportunity. Roger's defence—and he had the best Toronto lawyer money could buy—hardly bothered with the latter two. What family home didn't have a poisonous substance stored somewhere on the premises? What husband didn't have ample opportunity to murder his wife, if so inclined?

The whole case hung on motive. Roger, the defence insisted, had none. Granted, he had had an affair with me, a cheap liaison. Admitting that much, Roger expressed remorse and shame at having violated his own and his family's standards. It was untypical of the way he had thitherto led his life. I, the *femme fatale*, had seduced him. But to murder his wife in order to marry a caterer? The idea was ludicrous. Although I had suggested it, even pressured him, at no time had he intended to make me his wife.

He went on like that, admitting that he had taken me to motels. But not to his home. Never.

That lie was his downfall. The Crown jumped on it. "If you never took her to your home, then she could not have been the person who put poison into the vodka."

Roger backtracked. Suddenly he did remember the September night when Rosalind was in Vancouver and the brunch that I, alone in the kitchen, had prepared. I could have done it then.

"Can you produce any witness prepared to testify that your lover was in your home that night?"

"No."

Caught in a lie, Roger lost credibility.

Our romance made headlines as The Catered Affair. Roger's lawyer made cracks about hot canapés and hors d'oeuvres, which made the gallery titter but annoyed the judge. The jury, unimpressed by wealth and birth, appeared disgusted at Roger's attempt to shift the blame to me. "Guilty" was the unanimous verdict. Roger was sentenced to life in prison, without eligibility for parole for twenty-five years.

My trial came next. I had a local defence lawyer, Mr. W. T. Spark, well-known in Kingston for his success against B & E and drunk driving charges.

"I'll look after the evidence and the legal arguments," he said. "You look after your image. Bellamy has portrayed you as a scheming gold digger with social ambitions. Now it's up to you to show the judge and jury what real class is all about." He gave a wry smile. "We're lucky that Finkelman is judging your case. He has no great liking for the Old Stones of Kingston. His mother was a Holocaust survivor, and he certainly doesn't have five generations buried in Cataraqui Cemetery."

So there I sat in the prisoner's box, wearing my grey silk suit, my hair in a smooth chignon, pearls about my neck. In Judge Finkelman's eyes I recognized admiration and respect. Perhaps he saw in my rise to success something of his own struggles. Kingston's upper crust had also rejected him.

"Relax," Mr. Spark whispered. "Establish eye contact with the jurors. Avoiding it makes you look guilty. The evidence against you isn't strong. If you get the jury on your side, they're more likely to acquit."

But the jury—seven women and five men—was not on my side. I saw that from the start. Frowns. Pursed lips. "Uppity woman," their eyes said. "Home wrecker." "She must have egged him on."

Mr. Spark decided to put me on the stand. "You'll be a good witness. Just stick to your story."

So I swore that the only time I had ever been in the Bellamy home was to cater a ladies-only social event many months before my affair with Roger began. At that time, I obviously possessed no motive for conspiring to murder Mrs. Bellamy.

Mr. Justice Finkelman glanced at his notes. "And you were never in the Bellamy home between September 9 and September 21, when Mrs. Bellamy was out of town?"

"Certainly not."

"You may step down."

Then the legal arguments began—dozens and dozens of legal points, and as many angles from which to view the evidence. I saw jury members looking out the Courthouse windows at the wild geese flying south. By the time the judge was ready to give his direction to the jury, their eyes had glazed over.

I may have been the only person really listening by the time he finished his address to the jury.

"If you find that the accused knew of the perpetrator's intention to commit murder and encouraged him in pursuit of that object, then the accused may be party to the offence of conspiring even though she played no part in carrying out the offence. The ultimate determination of guilt is for you alone. Yet keep this in mind: even if you find sufficient evidence against the accused to consider her participation probable, that fact does not make a conviction automatic. The Crown must establish its case beyond a reasonable doubt."

The only thing I saw established beyond a reasonable doubt was the jury's dislike of me. It took them one hour to reach a verdict. "Guilty as charged," the foreman announced with grim satisfaction.

Mr. Justice Finkelman frowned. He acknowledged that the evidence was capable of supporting that verdict, but he did not thank the jury for its work.

I spent the next seven years in the Federal Prison for Women, Kingston's notorious P4W. It's closed now. I was one of the last to do time there. I still have nightmares about the ranges of cells with their steel bars, the depressing work-rooms where I sewed mailbags for seven years.

Roger is serving his sentence at one of those penal hotels for the rich. It even has a golf course. But I'm out of prison now, and he isn't. What happens to Roger is irrelevant. We'll never see each other again.

Burlington would have been a good place to start over. I'm beginning to get a sense of the city. Here, the people with money have more lavish tastes than my old Kingston clientele, and it's new, ambitious money. In one more year, I would have been ready to launch a small, prestige catering service of my own. I was going to call it Golden Apple. Both words are loaded with positive associations. But it isn't going to happen.

My boss eyes me queerly. "Marlene," she says, "we need to talk."

Red Dress must have got to her. Well, there's no help for it. In the catering business, presentation is everything. Conviction for conspiracy to murder by poison looks bad on a résumé.

In the Chambers
of the Sea

It was me that killed Zoë Post. Five years ago. Five years and two months. I used to count how many days it was too. Now that I'm getting over her, I don't keep track the way I used to. So far, I've gotten away with it. When the police went after the stalker, they hardly even looked at me.

Zoë and me went to Odessa High School at the same time. She was smarter than me, in the Smart Kids' Program. She could have gone to university. I was in the General Program like most of the other farm kids. Twelve years of schooling was as much as any of us needed. After graduation, we'd have farms to work and someday take over— farms that had been in the family for two hundred years. That meant bugger all to snobs like Zoë. They thought farming was just hoeing dirt and shovelling shit.

Zoë lived in Riverview, not a real town, just a fancy sub-division that some developer plunked down beside Cudney Creek. About a hundred kids from Riverview went to Odessa High School, every one of them a snob. The rest of us didn't have nothing to do with them. Zoë was as much a snob as every other Riverview kid, except when it came to music.

It was music that got me and her together. When we were all in our senior year of high school, me and Kyle and Laverne had this band, Smokin' Grass. I banged drums, Kyle played bass, and Laverne picked lead and did most of the singing too.

The principal, Mr. Asselstine, said we couldn't be in the school variety show with a name like Smokin' Grass. He called us into his office. If he'd made us stand up the whole time, we'd know we were in trouble. But he had three chairs already set out. Mr. Asselstine put on his uncle act—his "I was once young myself" routine—and talked about old-fash-ioned values. He came from around here, same as we did, except he'd gone off to university and then come back. Mr. Asselstine was Laverne's third cousin, two or three times removed. His grandpa and our great-grandpas used to go out to the barn and drink hard liquor whenever women took over the house for a quilting bee. We knew all about it. He knew we knew.

"Look, boys." Mr. Asselstine leaned back in his chair and looked us in the eye one by one. "I know you're just having fun. Smokin' Grass is a good name. But you can't use it here. I've already had an earful from the Chairman of the Board of Education. And look, I'll be frank with you: I want your band in the school variety show. I heard you play at the Napanee Fair last fall. I like your music. But you have to change your name."

So we got ourselves a second name, Amazing Grace, and learned a few Jesus songs. Amazing Grace played at weddings and county fairs. Smokin' Grass played the clubs. Everyone knew it was the same band. Nobody cared.

Laverne's family was religious, so it was through him we got roped into playing—for no pay—at the Strawberry Social that the United Church puts on every year. Quite a few Riverview people belonged to that church, so I wasn't surprised to see Zoë Post sitting there with a middle-aged couple and a girl about twelve with braces and straight blond hair. I knew she must be Zoë's sister, because in five years she was going to look like Zoë, if not as beautiful. Zoë was so beautiful it sucked the wind from your lungs. Sea-green eyes. Blond hair that hung perfectly straight to her shoulders. She was tall and slim, with a slender neck, and skin as pale as moonlight.

Zoë sat listening to our first set, but never smiled. Either she didn't like country rock or she was mad because her parents had dragged her to this boring church thing.

But during our break, while we huddled around a picnic table gobbling strawberry shortcake, Zoë walked over to us.

"Hi!" she said. "May I sit down?"

Laverne and Kyle just nodded because their mouths were crammed full of cake and strawberries. But I said, "Sure."

"You know," she said as she flipped her hair off her face, "you guys are really good. You ought to make a CD."

"We're thinking about it," I said. Thinking about it was all we could do, because we knew our gig pay wouldn't stretch to anything like that. And if we did get a hold of some money, we'd use it to buy half-decent equipment.

"You're good enough," she said, "except for one thing. Excuse me for saying so, but you need to find a singer."

"Yeah," I said, "we've been thinking about that too." Laverne choked on his cake. Kyle and I liked Laverne, but he had a range of about four notes. He sang pretty good most of the time, but not as good as he thought.

"I can sing," she said. "I've taken lessons."

"Yeah, but can you sing our kind of music?" Laverne said, spraying her with cake crumbs.

She turned those sea-green eyes on him high beam. "I can sing any kind. I write my own stuff too."

Kyle narrowed his eyes as if he thought somebody was trying to pull the wool over them. "Let's hear you."

"When?"

"Now."

She looked around at all the United Church people eating their strawberry shortcake and shook her head. "I need my guitar."

"Sunday. Three o'clock," I said. "In Kyle's barn. You know where that is?"

"Outside Yarker?"

"You got it."

Then me and Kyle and Laverne went back to do our next set. Laverne was grumpy all evening. He hardly even spoke to me, but I knew he'd come round. He was hell picking lead, when we could get him to focus.

The part of the barn where we practised used to be the milk shed, but since Kyle's dad went over to beef cattle, he let us have it. There was a nice dairy smell about it, milky but not sour. We had pushed the old cream separator over against the wall to make room.

On Sunday afternoon, Zoë showed up right on time. She took her guitar out of its case and got down to work without any small talk. What a voice! Like Joni Mitchell, but better. Her high notes soared—fluty, like a Baltimore oriole. And her low notes plunged, like a growl in the pit of your stomach.

Her best song was about mermaids singing to each other:

I have seen them riding seaward on the waves
Combing the white hair of the waves blown back
When the wind blows the water white and black.

We have lingered in the chambers of the sea
By sea-girls wreathed with seaweed red and brown
Till human voices wake us, and we drown.

On that last word her voice finally did hit bottom. You could imagine it was the ocean floor, and practically see all that seaweed waving in the currents. Her music made me shiver.

"I love those lyrics," I said. "Did you write them?"

"No. I took them from a poem we studied in English class."

She looked so smug saying that, just reminding me that we weren't in the same class, even at school.

"They're good," I said, "but we don't want to break any copyright laws."

"Don't worry. The poem was published in 1917. I'm careful about that sort of thing."

After she'd sung a couple more songs, I said we'd get back to her. But Kyle and Laverne spoke right up.

"Hold on, Dave," said Laverne, "I'm not that crazy about being lead singer. Zoë is terrific. If she joins us, we'll kick ass from Oshawa to Ottawa."

"Maybe across Canada," Kyle added.

I was feeling grouchy about her showing off with the poetry. "Okay. She can join us. But she has to change her name."

"Why should I?" she asked.

"Most people don't know how to say a name like Zoë. They'll call you Zoo, or maybe Zoy to rhyme with toy, or Zoe, to rhyme with toe. It's a dumb name."

"When I'm a star, everybody will know how to pronounce my name. There'll be thousands of baby girls named after me." Zoë was right. She would have been a star, given time.

Anyway, we let her keep her name.

At graduation I sat across the aisle from Zoë. She watched the valedictorian up on stage, but I don't think she was listening to his speech. Her head was angled slightly to one side, as if she was trying to catch the words of a distant song. When I looked at her, I felt like I could hear the music too.

None of our parents liked what we were going to do next. But we were eighteen years old and we'd finished high school. They couldn't have stopped us if they'd tried.

Mr. and Mrs. Post gave Zoë a blue Mazda for a graduation present. Me and Kyle and Laverne put our money together for a used van to carry our equipment.

Right from the start, we got as many gigs as we could handle. Within three months we'd made enough to buy new equipment. We played in Picton, Belleville, Kingston, Brockville. Then, as we got better known, we toured to Ottawa, Windsor, Hamilton, even Toronto. For Kyle, Laverne and me, Toronto was big time. Zoë seemed unimpressed.

There wasn't room for all of us in the van, so we took turns riding in the Mazda with Zoë. This was for her safety and for taking turns at the wheel.

Kyle and Laverne were in love with her. I was too, though there were things about her that I hated. Zoë wasn't in love with anyone.

If one of us guys was looking for a lay, we knew without being told that it wasn't going to be her.

Late September. We were on our way from Hamilton, where we'd had a Friday night gig at La Luna, to Windsor for a club booking that started the next night. Two rooms reserved at the Holiday Inn. Zoë always had a room to herself, us guys got twin beds and a cot. We expected to check in by four in the morning, then sleep until noon.

I was driving the Mazda when fog rolled in about three in the morning. It was what my dad would call a pea-souper. I couldn't see six feet in front of the car. Switching to high beams made it worse. The fog reflected the headlight beams so all I could see was one big glow. We slowed to a crawl. The van was somewhere ahead, but I couldn't see its tail lights.

"We better get off the freeway," I said, "or some transport will plough us."

"There's an exit just ahead. I couldn't make out the sign. But it said one kilometre."

"Good."

I hunched over the steering wheel, peered into all that whiteness, trying to find the dotted line that's painted on the right-hand side to show the turnoff lane. I'd just found it when a transport roared by. It passed with a rush and a glow out of the fog and into the fog again. The Mazda shuddered as it went by.

I inched along the exit road, stopped at a stop sign, and turned right onto some kind of secondary highway. Zoë peered through the fog looking for a motel. Before long she spotted the glow of a neon sign, and we turned in to the parking lot. Everyone on that stretch of the 401 must have had the same idea.

At the front desk, a middle-aged man was handing a key to a couple who looked just as relieved as me and Zoë to be off the road. "Number 12," he said to them, and they headed out the door.

"Have you got two rooms?" Zoë asked.

"Only one left."

"Twin beds?"

"One double."

"We'll take it," I said, before Zoë had a chance to say anything. "I'll sleep on the floor. You can have the bed."

Outside, another car pulled up. I felt sorry for the poor guy. At least me and Zoë had a room.

Our unit was Number 13. I didn't know whether that was unlucky or not, and I still haven't made up my mind. It sure didn't start good, because as soon as I took my shoes off I could feel water squish between my toes.

"They must have just shampooed the carpet. Sleeping on the floor is out."

"Try the armchair."

I cast an envious look in the direction of the bed. It was big enough for two.

"Dave, I know what you're thinking," she said. "And the answer is no."

Zoë said it was lucky she had her suitcase in the car and not the van. She went into the bathroom to change, and when she came out she was wearing a green plaid flannelette nightshirt with a ruffle around the neck. Maybe that doesn't sound sexy to you, but it drove me wild.

She climbed right into bed as natural as could be, just as if I wasn't there. Or maybe a skinny, middle-sized farm boy didn't count as a man, in her eyes.

My luggage was in the van, so I didn't have any choice but to sleep in my clothes. After I'd washed, I settled into the armchair. It was comfortable enough, as armchairs go. But it didn't recline, and I couldn't find anywhere to put my feet. Zoë's suitcase was too low, and the desk chair was too high. So I just sprawled there. After a couple of minutes, Zoë turned off the bedside light.

It's hard to sleep in an armchair. If your head flops down on your chest, you get a crick in your neck. If you let your head fall back, your mouth stays open and you snore. I woke myself up half a dozen times with a big croak like I was choking. Each time it happened, I woke up Zoë too.

"I can't stand this," she said. "Your snoring sounds like a helicopter. You better come sleep in the bed."

I got up, stumbled over, and started to climb in.

"Take off your jeans and shirt. You may as well be comfortable."

So I took them off, as well as my socks, which were wet from the carpet. As soon as I got into the bed, I rolled over so that my back was to her. But I could still feel her warmth and hear her breathing, fast and shallow. She wasn't asleep, though maybe she was pretending to be, because she didn't say anything.

I figured that she was nervous, having me in the same bed with her. So I lay real still. Then all at once I felt a gentle touch on the back of my neck, then fingers tracing down my spine, then Zoë's arm around my waist pulling me over on my back. Her fingertips drew little circles on my belly, but I didn't make a move. All sorts of things I might say were running through my mind, everything from "I love you" to "I hope you have a condom because I don't." But I didn't say them because she might reconsider, and I wanted her like I never wanted anything in my whole life.

If a voice—God's or somebody like that—told me I'd die and go to hell tomorrow to pay for this, it would have been okay by me.

Zoë didn't say nothing either, just let out a little sigh as she pulled herself close to me. Through her flannelette nightshirt I felt her soft, warm breasts against my chest. Wisps of her hair brushed my cheek, and her skin smelled like roses. I slid my hand up her thigh, just hoping I was doing it right.

When I woke up, I heard the shower running. I rolled over and laid there waiting for the bathroom door to open, imagining how Zoë would come out naked, or maybe with just a towel around her hips, and how she'd get back into bed with me. And after we'd made love, I'd tell her how I wanted to sleep with her every night for the rest of my life.

But when she came out, she was all dressed, wearing her jeans and a shirt, with her hair laying smooth and shiny on her shoulders. She didn't say a thing about last night. Maybe she was embarrassed, though she didn't look it. I thought I'd better say something, because she had to know this was the greatest thing that ever happened to me. But suddenly I got tongue-tied, and I couldn't even look her in the eye.

"About last night …" I said.

"It doesn't matter. Forget it." As if I could!

From then on I had to act as if it hadn't happened, and Zoë acted the same. Yet I couldn't look at her without remembering the softness of her breasts and the way she drew me into her. If she didn't want to talk about it, I wasn't going to force her. But she knew—she had to know—that she was mine for life.

A month later, the four of us were on the road again, having breakfast at the Comfort Inn in North Bay, when Zoë broke the news. She was leaving us, moving to Toronto. She had an agent. Everything was arranged. Seems she had gone to a recording studio to make her own CD without telling us.

"Why didn't you make your CD with us?" I spluttered. But I knew why. Zoë planned to go places where me and Laverne and Kyle were never going to go.

Laverne patted her on the back. "That's great, Zoë, we'll come and hear you at Roy Thomson Hall."

Kyle looked at her over the rim of his coffee cup, and I'd swear there were tears in his eyes. "Zoë, you got a voice that will take you as far as you want to go."

"I'll keep in touch," she said. "I won't forget that Smokin' Grass is where I began."

After that, we didn't talk about it much. There were a couple gigs we had to do before Zoë left. But in her own mind she'd already gone. She'd stare into space with a long-distance look in her eyes. Where was she in her thoughts? Not just Toronto. New York, Las Vegas, London—the world was waiting for her. She knew it. We knew it.

Things weren't the same after Zoë left. Laverne went back to being lead singer until we got a new vocalist named Jenny. Laverne and Kyle liked her, and I could see why. She wasn't like Zoë. Bouncy and friendly is how I'd describe her. She was short, with dark hair, brown eyes, and a wide mouth that smiled a lot. Laverne and Kyle used to kid around with her, but I never did.

Sometimes, after practice, I'd take my brushes and swish out the rhythm of Zoë's mermaid song. When I did that, I could hear her voice singing as if she was right there beside me:

> *We have lingered in the chambers of the sea*
> *By sea-girls wreathed with seaweed red and brown*
> *Till human voices wake us, and we drown.*

Drown. That deep note sounding from the bottom of the sea. I wish she'd told me the poet's name so I could look it up. Then I could talk to her about poetry and stuff after we got married.

Six months after she left us, in early spring Zoë came home for a visit. I bumped into her walking down Odessa's main street, which is practically its only street. She was on the opposite sidewalk, coming toward me. I did a double take when I saw her. It was Zoë all right, but she had glamour now. Not that she was more beautiful, but everything about her—hair, skin, eyes, clothes—looked polished. As soon as she saw me, she smiled and crossed right over.

"Dave! This is great! I just came home for a couple of days to see my folks. I was planning to phone you."

"When are you going back to Toronto?"

"Tomorrow morning."

From that, it didn't sound as if she planned to spend much time with me.

"What about a coffee?" I said.

"Sure."

So we went into the lunch bar that's attached to Macdonald's Service Station. I bought coffee and a couple of donuts, and we sat down at one of them little tables with our knees bumping together.

"I miss you," I said.

"I miss you too."

She sounded as if she meant it. I almost got up my nerve to tell her how I went to sleep every night thinking about her, and how her voice floated in my head like I was one of those guys that lingered in the chambers of the sea. But I could never say stuff like that.

We finished our coffee, and she was wiping donut crumbs from her lips when all of a sudden she said, "Come and see me in Toronto."

"Sure. Where do you live?"

"The Bromleigh. It's near Bloor and Bay."

"Sounds like a hotel."

"It is. The first twenty floors are hotel rooms, but the top two are apartments. I'm on the twenty-first floor."

"When do you want me to come?"

"Sometime in the summer." Zoë opened her handbag, took a card out of a little case, and handed it to me.

The card was cream coloured with raised letters: REITMAN AGENCY. In the lower left corner was a name, Clara Chown, with a phone number, fax number and e-mail address.

"Who's this?" I asked.

"My agent. Get in touch with her."

"Why do I have to call your agent?"

"Stalkers." She shrugged. "It happens. I need to be careful. For safety, Clara arranges all my appointments. She knows my schedule. Tell her who you are and ask her to fix a date. Any free afternoon will be fine."

"Yeah, but you know me. I'm no stalker."

She smiled. "No exceptions. Even for old friends."

I nearly choked. Who did Zoë think she was? The Queen?

Zoë closed her handbag and stood up. We left the lunch bar together. Out on the sidewalk, she lifted her face to kiss me. When I felt those soft lips brush my cheek, I didn't know whether to put my arms around her or punch her in the head.

The agent's card stayed in my wallet for about two weeks until I threw it out. I was damned if I was going to make an appointment to see Zoë, as if it was a trip to the dentist. I knew where she lived.

By August I couldn't stand it any longer. I had to see her and get things sorted out. It was a quiet month for Smokin' Grass. In fact, most months had been quiet since Zoë left. Jenny had to take a part-time job waitressing. Laverne and Kyle were helping their dads with the harvest. I was living in Kingston, which is the nearest city to Odessa, sort of looking for a job. Smokin' Grass didn't have any gigs lined up for the next couple of weeks.

On August 15—that was the day—I bought a one-way train ticket to Toronto. One way was all I needed. Maybe I wouldn't be coming back, at least not for a long time. If I could just spend two or three days with Zoë, she'd see how much she needed me.

The train from Kingston to Toronto goes right by Odessa, so I was looking out the window as we passed our old high school, and then the United Church where Amazing Grace—we hadn't used that name for over a year—had played at the Strawberry Social. That's the church where we'd get married, Zoë and me.

As the train carried me further and further, I leaned back in my seat and watched the flat farmlands give way to the rolling hills of Northumberland County, and all the time Zoë was on my mind. I had this dream that I could be Zoë's manager. Well, why not? Céline Dion had René Angélil, and Shania Twain had Mutt Lange. I could book gigs, reserve hotel rooms, make phone calls, do Zoë's income tax. She wouldn't need an agent if she had me.

I figured that Smokin' Grass would find another drummer without too much trouble. The Beatles had changed drummers; Laverne and Kyle could too. All the way to Toronto, I dreamed about how great the future was going to be.

The train stopped with a soft bump. Union Station. This is it, I said to myself. I felt jittery thinking how close I was to being with Zoë. My hands were cold and clammy, and I kept wiping my palms on my pant legs. For a few minutes I stayed in my seat while the other passengers picked up their bags. Then I got my backpack from the overhead rack and left the train.

I took the subway north to Bloor, then walked the rest of the way. The Bromleigh was a fancy hotel, but not super fancy. A uniformed doorman stood at the curb, waving down a taxi. He didn't see me as I went through the revolving door.

The lobby was awesome. High ceilings. Chandeliers. Easy chairs with leather upholstery. I chose a chair that would give me a good view of the elevators. The idea of asking for her at the desk made me nervous. Watching and waiting seemed more natural. Whether she was up in her apartment or out somewhere, Zoë would have to use the elevator sooner or later.

I sat for an hour, watching the elevator doors open and close, seeing people get in or come out. There were four elevators. The one at the left end of the row had a brass sign above it: Express to Residential Floors. That's the elevator Zoë would take. Dozens of people took the other three. They kept on going up and down all the time, but hardly anyone used the express. Every time the light above its door blinked its way down towards the lobby, I held my breath. Then the door would open and some guy in an expensive suit would come out, or some lady wearing snakeskin shoes with four-inch heels and carrying a big purse that matched.

Would Zoë be wearing high-heel shoes? That would make her as tall as me, and I wouldn't like that. Worse still, she might walk out of that elevator holding the arm of one of those suits. And if she did, then what would I do?

I was really starting to sweat by the time Zoë stepped out of the elevator. She wasn't dressed up at all. Flat sandals. Blue jeans. T-shirt. And her blond hair loose to her shoulders. She glanced quickly to the right and to the left, and then made a beeline across the lobby.

When she saw me jump out of my chair and start towards her, she stopped in her tracks. Her face went white, like she was scared. Then she laughed and held out both hands.

"Dave! What a nice surprise!" Again she looked around real quick, as if she thought somebody might be watching. "I just came down to buy some toothpaste. Let me get it, then we'll go up to my apartment so we can talk and have a beer."

There was a convenience store off the lobby, along with a gift shop and a barbershop. I stood at the postcard rack while she bought her toothpaste. "Let's go," she said as soon as she had paid for it. Her eyes darted this way and that while we crossed the lobby to the elevators.

As soon as we got onto the express elevator and the door closed, she let out her breath.

"What's the problem?" I asked. "You looked kind of worried down there."

"Somebody is stalking me. I think I told you. He sends me flowers and little notes. I don't know who he is."

"What do the notes say?"

"That he loves me."

"That sounds creepy."

"It is. The police take it seriously. He orders the flowers from a different florist each time and he always pays cash. That makes him hard to trace."

When we got to the twenty-first floor, she looked both ways along the corridor, then didn't waste any time getting to her apartment.

I didn't think much of Zoë's apartment. It had that same beige look of all the motels I've ever stayed in. She showed me around: kitchenette, bathroom, bedroom. That was all.

"It's what I need," she said. "A home base in Toronto. This apartment might not look like much, but it costs a fortune."

"It's nice," I said.

A round coffee table sat in front of a pair of easy chairs, angled side by side. I sat down while she went into the kitchen to pour the beer.

The walls of her apartment were bare except for one big poster—a photograph of tall trees, like they have in B.C. or California. It looked dark and deep under the trees. So real I felt like I could take Zoë's hand and step right into the forest to go for a walk.

Under the poster, a table stood against the wall. On it were a pair of brass candlesticks and two framed photographs. I recognized Zoë's parents and kid sister in one. The other picture was a dark-haired guy about our age. He wasn't anyone I knew.

Zoë brought us each a glass of beer, then sat down in the other armchair, her legs tucked up beside her.

She kept her eyes on me while she sipped her beer. Zoë never did have much to say. She didn't chatter all the time, like some girls, jabbering about their friends and clothes.

Being quiet like that made her kind of mysterious. She had her head tilted to one side. Maybe she was listening to music that I couldn't hear.

She gave her head a little shake, as if to wake herself up. "Dave, it's so great to see you."

She gave me a big smile, but it didn't match the anxious look in her eyes. Under her relaxed manner, I could see that Zoë was nervous. She shouldn't be living by herself. There were all kinds of weirdos in Toronto. If she had me to protect her, that stalker would leave her alone. Or I'd sort him out.

"What brings you to T.O.?"

"I came to see you." This was the moment to get serious, to tell her how much I needed her and she needed me. I didn't know where to start.

"That's sweet," she said. "I always love to see any of the old high school gang. You, Laverne, Kyle. You're like family."

I felt a spurt of anger. She shouldn't have lumped me in with Kyle and Laverne. I wasn't family, at least not in the way she said it.

She set down her beer on the coffee table. "Remember how we used to practise in Kyle's cow barn? We had a good time, didn't we?" She laughed. "Remember the gigs at county fairs, and the church socials?"

Was it memories she wanted? Maybe that was how to reach her. I leaned toward her, looked into her eyes.

"Remember that foggy night on the way to Windsor, when I tried to sleep on a chair like this one?"

"Yeah."

She looked uncomfortable, as if she wished I wouldn't bring up that subject. But I wasn't going to pretend it hadn't happened. "We made love that night. It's something we'll always share."

Zoë picked up her glass, staring into it as if some insect was floating in her beer. A red flush spread up her neck and turned her pale cheeks pink.

"Don't make it into something big. We had sex. It didn't mean anything."

"To me it meant something."

"Dave, I've always liked you. That wouldn't have happened if I didn't, but ..." She raised her hand to sweep her hair off her face.

"Do that again," I said.

"Do what?"

"With your fingers—the way you brushed your hair back, like the mermaid in your song. You know: "Combing the white hair of the waves blown back ..."

She sang the next line. Actually sang it with that sweet, thrilling voice: "When the wind blows the water white and black."

"Yeah. In the chambers of the sea."

Zoë stood up, and walked over to the window. "That's a different world."

I crossed the room to join her. Far below us the traffic was gridlocked on Bloor Street, bumper to bumper. Pedestrians, flowing in streams towards the nearest subway station, moved faster than the cars. To the west lay the university campus, green as a forest, with buildings sticking up through the trees. Off to the left, I saw the CN Tower in the distance.

"Is this your world now?" I asked.

"Yes."

"Then it's my world too."

I heard the sharp intake of her breath. As she turned to me, I felt the soft touch of her fingers on my arm. I leaned closer. Now I could kiss her. This was the moment, with those wonderful sea-green eyes, deep as forever, looking into mine. My skin tingled where her fingers rested on my arm.

"Dave, you're one of the greatest guys I've ever met. But there's no place for you in the life I lead now."

It was like she slammed a door in my face. No place for me? What was she talking about? I heard my voice go hoarse and shaky. "Don't say that. Wherever you are, that's where I belong. I belong to you, and you belong to me. It's time you understood that."

She lifted her hand from my arm, stepped back. "Dave …" Her face went tight. "There's nothing between us. You shouldn't have barged in on me. If you can't accept that we're just friends, I don't want to see you again."

She folded her arms across her chest. From the look in her eyes, there could have been a barbed wire fence between us.

"Zoë, listen to me. You may think I'm only a hick you knew from Odessa High School, but I can make you a star. There's no limit to what I can do for you."

"What could you possibly do for me?"

"I got you here, didn't I?"

"You got me here!" she sneered. "That's the funniest thing you've said yet."

I didn't intend to grab her, at least not as hard as I did. She needed me to give her a little shake, and I was getting mad.

"You'd better leave." Her lips trembled. She was scared.

"No. I'm not leaving." My hands gripped her shoulders. Tight. "You're going to hear what I have to say. I didn't come all the way from Odessa to be treated like a piece of shit."

"Odessa isn't that far," she snapped. I could see what an ugly mood she was in, but that wasn't going to stop me.

"Shut up and listen," I told her, "I got a plan for us. It's like this. You need a manager. All the big stars got managers. Look what René Angélil did for Céline Dion. He made her what she is. I can do the same for you. We'll be like Shania Twain and Mutt Lange. You'll be big. Really big. Right up there with Avril Lavigne and Sylvia Tyson and Gordon Lightfoot. I'll handle publicity. Get you onto *The Oprah Winfrey Show*." I knew I was talking too fast, but the words kept spilling out. "I'll handle your recording contracts, get you bookings in New York, Los Angeles."

"Who do you know in New York or L.A.? Who do you know anywhere?" She pulled away from me, and brushed her shoulders with her fingertips as if I'd left dirt on her.

"Next month I'll be recording in Memphis for a label with a head office in California. My agent has my first European tour arranged for next spring. London, Paris, Zurich, Vienna …" She laughed, short and hard. Like a bark. "Maybe I can take you on as a roadie. You can sell souvenirs."

She looked at me like I was a barn rat. Then she said, real quiet, "I'm sorry, but I really have to ask you to leave. I'm going out for dinner and need to get ready. My boyfriend is picking me up in an hour."

A shiver went through me. I got the feeling that I'd lost control, like when you're driving on ice and the car spins right around. That was when I blew up. I saw in a flash everything that I hadn't wanted to see. Zoë was a bitch. She let me make love to her one night because she was in the mood and I happened to be there. She thought she could stomp all over my heart and then just wave *bye-bye*.

My stomach clenched like I was about to throw up. A bitter taste rose at the back of my mouth. My arms hung at my sides. I clenched and unclenched my fists, imagining the feel of them around her soft, silky throat. I could wring her neck like a chicken's.

She backed away a couple of steps, looking real scared, and I thought: she's going to scream. I went for her before she could.

There was terror in those sea-green eyes. If my hands hadn't been squeezing her throat, she would have screamed. And I couldn't have stood that, to hear Zoë scream. So I squeezed harder and harder until her body slumped and there was no more life in her eyes than in two glass marbles.

I picked her up and carried her to the bed. Gently I laid her down and sat beside her. I remembered making love to her in the motel that foggy night. I kissed her on the lips and stroked her hair. "Zoë," I said, "this isn't how it was supposed to be."

I had to get out of there, because the guy she called her boyfriend would be there in half an hour. I washed my beer glass and put it back in the cupboard, went around the apartment with a dishcloth, wiped off everything I might have touched. Then I left.

No one was in the elevator. I walked across the hotel lobby and through the revolving door without turning around. There are advantages in being the sort of guy that no one notices. I took the 6:30 bus back to Kingston and got home in three hours.

I was sure that I'd be a suspect. The police interviewed me, just like they interviewed Kyle and Laverne. The police didn't find out I'd been in Toronto that day. They didn't know that Zoë and me had been lovers. Not even Kyle and Laverne knew that.

The police found the guy who'd been stalking Zoë, and charged him with murder. When it came to trial, he was acquitted. I was glad of that. If he'd been convicted, I was going to confess. I might have, too.

A Quick
Release

I slip into the seat beside Mike Stonehouse as the train
pulls out of Union Station. After four pints of Molson
Golden in the station bar, I have a nice buzz. Last night we
beat Hamilton, my old team, in the CFL Eastern Semi-Final.
The Voyageurs don't win all that often in the playoffs. Hell,
they don't get to the playoffs that often. It's been a while
since I've seen a decent chance of going all the way to Grey
Cup.

Mike's looking at a photograph held in his big hands.
Mike has good hands. Long fingers. All bone and tendon.
Never drops a ball, except when he starts to run before he's
got a firm grip. That's a rookie fault. There's a smirk on Mike's
face. I'm curious about the photograph, but don't try to see
what it is. What pictures a man looks at are his own business.

He recognizes me and smiles. Mike's a good-looking kid. Curly black hair. Broad shoulders.

"That was a great pass," he says.

"Great catch," I answer. "You were pretty well covered. I didn't think there was much chance you'd make it."

"Peter, we won the game. You and me. Hamilton never came back."

"Winning's always a team effort." I take the correct tone you do with a rookie so he won't get a swelled head.

"Yeah. Course it is." He looks back down at the photograph, no longer concealed by his hands. This time I look. It's a baby picture. Baby. Not babe. Little girl around two with a mop of dark curls, wearing one of those pint-size Voyageur sweatshirts. She's running toward the camera waving a single, red maple leaf.

"Cute," I say. "I didn't know you had a kid. Didn't know you were married."

Mike flushes bright pink. He's young enough to be embarrassed. Everyone knows he's screwing one of our cheerleaders.

"Wife's back in the Soo," he says. "I don't get home during football."

"Who does?" Then, to relax him, I say, "The rest doesn't matter, so long as you save the best for your wife."

"I'm cool with that." He slips the photo into an envelope and sticks it into his breast pocket.

He asks me, "Do you have kids?"

"One boy."

"How old?"

"Eleven." I'm pretty sure of that.

My mind drifts back ten years to the time when I was playing for Hamilton, a smart young quarterback beginning to get noticed. Not bad-looking, despite big ears. I remember striding up Balsam Avenue after morning practice one bright October day, crunching leaves under my feet, thinking about next weekend's football game and running over the game plan in my mind. That was the day I saw my son for the first time.

"Does he play football?" Mike asks

I do a double take. "Who? Oh, my son. I don't know. He lives with his mother."

Mike stops asking. Doesn't want to get too personal. I'm a veteran; he's a rookie. He drops the subject and looks out the window.

The train slows for Oshawa. Doesn't stop. Three whistle blasts, then up to speed. Again my thoughts drift back

Her name was Tracy. I don't remember her last name. She's married now. Different name anyway. Pretty girl, but nothing you'd especially notice. Light brown hair that hung straight down. Turned-up nose. Wide-set big brown eyes that gave her a Bambi look that was sort of cute. Nice smile.

I'd hardly given her a thought since we broke up. But there she was, walking up the sidewalk toward me, pushing a stroller. I didn't expect the stroller.

I was going to cross the street, but she caught sight of me. With her staring right at me, it might have seemed cowardly to cross the street. I wouldn't have wanted Tracy to think I was afraid to face her. The best thing to do was just carry on with my head up, and maybe nod casually. She seemed to have the same idea.

I was about to nod when Tracy said, "You asshole!" Right out loud.

What the hell! She didn't have to take that attitude! So I didn't nod, but I did sneak a peek at the baby. I don't know what I expected, but I wasn't surprised that the kid looked like me. Same broad cheekbones, pale freckled skin. Same big ears. Same red hair. Oh, yeah, I saw it all. I'm a quick read.

We're out in the country now. The train click-clicks along the rails. Farms and towns flash by. October is my favourite month, and not just because of football. The trees are wearing their colours—yellow, orange, red and brown.

Mike turns to me. "I'm going to the bar car. Want to join me?"

"Sure. Why not?" I don't like the bar car. Too smoky. But I could use another beer. Thinking about my kid always gets me down. Every time the Voyageurs play in Hamilton, I find myself looking for a red-haired boy with big ears. He might be riding his bike along the street or tossing a ball in a park. I don't mean I have a plan to find him. Nothing like that. But if I saw him I could ask his name. Or if there were other people around, I could inquire, "Who's that kid?" I could follow him home and write down the address. Tracy married a steelworker. One of my teammates who stayed in Hamilton year-round had told me that.

In the bar car, I have a Golden, and then another. We're only just past Port Hope. That means I've had six beers in two hours. Enough to make me mellow, loosen my tongue.

"Hey, Peter, you all right?"

"Sure." I rouse myself. "Just thinking about my life."

"Heavy."

Mike looks at me over the rim of his glass, seems interested. So I tell him.

"You know my style. When I throw the ball, I like to spread it around. I like plays where there are five or six receivers. I look them all over, stare straight at one particular guy, then throw the ball real fast to someone else."

"Yeah. You're good at that." He smiles.

"A quick read and a quick release," I say.

He orders a couple more beers, slides one across the Arborite to me.

I raise it to him. "When it comes to women, I operate the same way. Lots of receivers. A quick read and a quick release. I stare at one, then throw the ball to another. This girl, Tracy, was one I stared at. There were plenty others. Cheerleaders, nurses, physiotherapists, college students, waitresses—you name it."

Mike grins. "There's no shortage of pretty women. It blew my mind when I first joined the team. They hang around the stadium after games, come right up to you in pubs. They don't care whether a guy is married or single so long as he plays football."

"They keep score—same as we do," I say. "But there are rules to every game. And Tracy didn't understand. She got too serious. She started asking whether we might have a future together. When women ask that question, it's time to split. Like I said, a quick release.

"I told Tracy, 'I like you a lot. We've had some good times. But the fact is, I'm engaged to a girl back home in Pennsylvania. We're getting married right after Grey Cup.' Tracy took it bad. God! I hate it when they cry.

"Kathy was my intended receiver. I had her picked out right from the start. She was smart and beautiful. A tall blonde. Elegant. Tracy was never in her class."

Mike nods. He understands.

"Kathy got the wedding ring, but it was Tracy who got the baby. A couple of months after I'd broken up with Tracy, I found her waiting for me outside the players' door at the stadium. 'Pete,' she said, 'I have something to tell you. We're going to have a baby.' I said, 'Who's we?' She said, 'You and me.'

"I didn't say anything. I could see it was a big deal for her, and wasn't sure how she expected me to react. I guess she wanted me to jump up and down and hug her and say that we'd get married and quick. As she stared at me, those big Bambi eyes filled with tears. 'That's too bad, Tracy,' I said. 'Are you going to have an abortion?'

"Then she really started to cry. She didn't seem to understand that this was her business, not mine. It was embarrassing to have her standing there crying where the other guys could see her. I got kind of angry. Anyway, that was the last time I saw Tracy."

Mike says, "But she went ahead and had the baby?"

"That's right. How could I have known she'd do that? My son must have been born in the off-season when I was home in Pennsylvania. She could have let me know after I got back to Canada. I was still with the Tiger Cats for two more years before I became a free agent. She knew where to find me. I'd been a father for more than a year, and I didn't know."

"Just as well," Mike says. "She might have got you for child support."

"Which I could not afford at that time. But even then I thought about ways I could keep an eye on my kid. Maybe I could start by buying him a teddy bear. That might soften up Tracy so she'd let me come to visit him. Women like it when the father wants to be involved.

"Of course I couldn't let Kathy find out. She already feels bad enough because we can't have children. Her fault. Obviously not mine! But we have a good marriage, at least during the off-season. She has to stay in Pennsylvania year round because of her job."

I see that Mike isn't listening. His eyes are on two pretty girls that just came into the bar car. As they pass our table, the train gives a lurch and one of them bumps her hip against Mike's shoulder. It isn't necessary.

They're young—about nineteen. Both have long hair and delicate features. They remind me of Tracy, except these two are black around the eyes. Makeup, not kidney disease. One has a stud in her nose. They sit down at the table across the aisle.

Mike makes eye contact with both of them. They're not looking at me. It's all Mike. They lean their heads together, giggle. Maybe they're making a deal: who gets Mike and who gets the other one, the old guy.

"Shall we go over?" There's a gleam in Mike's eye.

"Nah. Not in the mood."

"Do you mind?" He is half out of his chair.

"Not in the least."

I debate whether to order another beer. Decide not to. I leave Mike in the bar car huddled with the girls, talking and laughing.

I go back where I'd been sitting before. Now I have the window seat. The train follows a long, slow curve around a bay as it slows for Kingston. I'm glad that Mike went to sit with the girls. If I'd stayed with him in the bar car much longer, I would have told him about today, about the boy in the park.

The boy was with his friends, half a dozen kids about the same age, eleven or twelve. I looked them over, not expecting better luck this time than any other. They were heading for the open ground beyond the flower beds, carrying a baseball, a bat, and various mitts.

They didn't notice me. I was just another adult sitting by the fountain, which was still spouting streams of water skyward even in October. The wind caught the spray and flung it in my direction. I got up to move, and that was when I noticed the kid. He took off his baseball cap and scratched his head. Red hair. Big ears.

I strolled up the gravel path in the same direction they were going, then left the path to walk on the grass, moving in closer. My heart beat fast. I watched for a clear look at his face, and then he turned toward me. It was him, all right. Even the freckles matched. Not one touch of Tracy. I saw myself, the way I was as a boy.

Did he know that I existed? Did my son realize that the man who raised him wasn't his father? He ought to know the truth. He'd be proud that his real daddy is a famous quarterback. Maybe not internationally famous, but well-known in Canada.

I watched the boys huddle, no doubt deciding what position each would play. From the opposite direction four more kids came across the park to join them.

I glanced at my watch. In one hour the chartered bus would leave from Ivor Wynne Stadium to take us to Toronto to board the train. Not much time. Not much choice. I had to find out the kid's name and then get to the stadium. The rest could be learned later through private investigation.

The huddle broke up. Each boy trotted off to take up position. "Put him in right field," I prayed. "Bring him this way so I can talk to him."

No such luck. He was standing around in front of home plate, holding the ball.

No help for it. I walked toward him, shouted, "Son, come over here. I need to talk to you."

He took a few steps in my direction, then stopped. His eyes, under the peak of his cap, were my eyes. Pale blue with a darker rim around the iris. I'm sure he saw it all—ears, cheekbones, hair—what was left of it—still red. When my eyes caught his, I saw recognition and fear. I hastened my steps toward him.

"What's your name?"

He tore his eyes away, looked down, shuffled his feet.

"Not allowed."

"What do you mean, not allowed?"

"Can't give my name to strangers."

Then one of the boys shouted, "Hey! Bernie! We can't start the game without a pitcher."

He spun around and loped across the grass. Pitcher, eh? Must have a good throwing arm, my son.

As I returned to the gravel path, a man came up to me. Middle-aged. Stocky build. Looked Italian.

"I seen you here before, watching the kids." His eyes locked on mine. There was a flicker of recognition. I better get away from here, I thought, before the penny drops.

"I'll call the cops," he said, "if I ever see you hanging around here again. Goddamn pervert."

I gave him a look that said I could knock his block off if I wanted to, then left the park.

Loss

I drive up and down Hillside Avenue for twenty minutes, looking for a place to park that will give me a clear view of the house without being too close. Then I sit watching through the rain-streaked windshield. Except for the porch light, no lights are showing. Two cars sit in the driveway: Clive's Passat and a red Neon that belongs to Ashley. I know it's hers because I've followed it many times.

My daughter Olivia also has a Neon, but it's not red. What colour is Olivia's car? Green? Blue? I don't remember. I was in hospital last time she visited from Ottawa, so of course I didn't see it. Actually, I think the colour is dark green. Olivia is a couple of years older than Ashley. Her taste is more mature.

It's raining hard. Maybe I should use my umbrella. I have

it in the car. But peeking into Clive's family room window with an open umbrella over my head would be absurd. He'd see me for sure, or Ashley would. If I had to run, it would get in my way. Better endure a wet wig than take unnecessary risks.

I keep my face lowered and hope no one notices me as I walk along the sidewalk and up the driveway. From the end of the driveway, fourteen stone steps lead down to the terrace. There is no railing. I keep my open palm against the stuccoed wall of the house as I descend.

When Clive and I designed the house, we had it built right into the side of the ravine. It looks like a bungalow from the front, but it's really a two-storey. The family room is downstairs at the back. That's where I'll find Clive and Ashley. Probably watching TV. There'll be a fire in the fireplace. Clive always lights a fire on a cold, rainy night like this. He enjoys a warm blaze and a snifter of brandy.

I creep around the corner at the bottom of the steps and pass the storage room door. Just ahead, the family room window is a bright rectangle of light. Pressing my body to the wall, I edge towards the window. Just as I reach it, I feel myself go weak.

It's not too late, I think, to change my mind. All I have to do is climb the steps, return to my car and drive off. But then I won't know what Clive and Ashley do when they're alone together. So I stick out my neck.

Outside, where I am, the glass is streaked with rain. Inside, where they are, a fire blazes. That's lucky. Firelight reflecting on glass turns the picture window into one huge mirror. I'd practically have to press my face against it to be seen. I can stand here as long as I like, almost safe, and watch them.

Clive reclines in the La-Z-Boy chair that I gave him for Christmas four years ago. From where I stand, I see him in half profile: grey hair, horn-rimmed glasses, one hand holding a brandy snifter. He's wearing his green cardigan. I gave him that too.

Ashley lies on the hearth rug, propped on her elbows, her chin resting in her hands. She is dressed in blue jeans and a black turtleneck. Her long, honey-coloured hair hangs free. She turns her head towards Clive. Ashley has a heart-shaped face with big luminous eyes, a small nose, and full lips.

She's facing me, but she doesn't see me. Still, I jump back instinctively, and my heart pounds. When I look again, Clive has set down his brandy. I hear his voice but can't make out his words. Ashley smiles, gets up, goes to him and crawls onto his lap. She puts her hand at the back of his neck and pulls his head down. She kisses him. I can't see Clive's face, only the curtain of Ashley's hair.

She starts squirming around, trying to straddle him. "Careful!" Clive's warning comes through the glass. The chair is at the point of toppling over. "Whoa! Just a minute!"

There's a clunk as the La-Z-Boy footrest goes down. Then the two of them spill onto the hearth rug, missing the fire screen by inches. They roll around, pawing each other. Hands grope, zippers unzip, clothing is pulled aside. Ashley's jeans and panties are off; Clive's trousers are around his ankles, and I have an unobstructed view of my former husband's rear end. In the firelight his buttocks are two pasty lumps, like bread dough after the first rise, when it's ready to be punched down.

I feel dizzy and sick. Well, what did I expect? I wanted to see what they do when they're alone. Now I see it. The spectacle of Clive's bare butt humping and pumping makes me want to throw up. I turn away from the window and crouch in the rain, shivering and retching, then creep away.

While I'm going by the storage room, my fingers find the latch on the door. Without thinking, I enter and close the door behind me. It feels good to be out the rain. The storage room smell comforts me. Mould, mouse dirt and mustiness, with a scent of lumberyard underneath from the stacked firewood. The smell hasn't changed.

Despite the darkness, I know where everything is. Clive keeps the hatchet on a nail just inside the door and the axe against the wall beside the chopping block.

When I remember the axe, a verse comes to me as clearly as if a voice spoke into my ear: "Lizzie Borden took an axe / And gave her mother forty whacks, / And when she saw what she had done / She gave her father forty-one." Why did she do it? I don't know. She must have suffered a great injustice, as I have suffered, felt pain as great as mine. I envy Lizzie Borden's rapture, the ecstasy of the avenging Fury, the blood flying everywhere.

Three steps deeper into darkness bring me to the axe. But it isn't in its usual place. Its blade has been struck into the chopping block, where it sticks like Excalibur in the stone. Though I tug with all my might, I cannot pull it out.

The hatchet, then? Easier for a woman to wield. My head fills with red and black as I tiptoe back to the door, grasp the hatchet and take it from the wall. The wooden shaft feels good in my hand. I raise it high, imagine the swift fall of the blade. Madame Guillotine. I shall burst into the family room, a warrior queen, swinging the hatchet with both hands. They'll beg for mercy, but I'll show none. Well, none to Ashley. Maybe when she's dead, Clive will love me again.

No, I think ruefully, that's not the way life works. Clive will never, ever love me again. I run my fingers over the hatchet blade, test its sharpness, then hang it back on the nail.

Leaving the storage room, I go back the way I came. On the street, the glare of headlights approaches from both directions through the slanting rain. Until the road is clear, I hide behind a spruce tree, then walk at a normal pace back to my car.

My key won't go in the lock. Jittery fingers fumble. My key ring falls on the street. I can't find it. There's rain on my glasses and rain on the road, making me half blind as I scrabble and grope on the wet pavement. I find my key ring in a puddle behind the front tire. This time it fits into the lock, and I realize that I had been trying to open the car door with the key to the trunk.

When I get into the car, I shake so hard my bones feel like they're coming apart. I grip the steering wheel and cling as if on a roller coaster ride. My mind replays the scene in the family room. Porn movie time, featuring Ashley Bimbo and Clive Moore. What will the next scene be? When do I make my entrance? Before the final fade out, I'll have my role to play. I turn the key in the ignition, and as the motor starts up, my mind fills with sudden knowledge that the last act is about to begin.

I drive with caution, like a party guest on his way home when he knows he's had too much to drink. Keep inside the speed limit. Halt at every stop sign and amber light. But does it matter if the police stop me? It isn't as if I've done anything wrong.

As soon as I get back to the apartment, I pull off my soaking wig and throw it on the floor. The face in the hall mirror scowls at me. The ugliest face I've ever seen: sunken cheeks, yellow skin, and a naked skull like a death's head. In Merrie Olde New England, they'd hang me for a witch.

My wig, lying on the parquet floor, is a raccoon that's been run over by a car. I pick it up, give it a shake, and carry it into my bedroom, where I keep the Styrofoam head that keeps it in shape when I'm not wearing it.

I make a cup of camomile tea and go to bed. In the medicine cabinet there are sleeping pills that my doctor prescribed, but I'm keeping them for future use. My breast throbs. My left breast, that is—the one that isn't there. I wonder what the hospital did with my severed breast. Burned it? They must have burned it, unless they threw it out in the garbage or preserved it in a bottle of formaldehyde for the purpose of instructing students.

I signed a paper giving the hospital permission to dispose of any body parts that I would never use again. Now I wish

I hadn't. I should have asked to keep my breast. I could have held a funeral for it. Depart, O Christian breast, out of this world, in the name of the babes that suckled at thee (two, to be precise), in the name of the lovers that fondled thee (three or four, but so long ago that I forget their names). Alas, poor breast! I could have buried you and planted a rose bush on your grave.

In a few months they'll have a funeral for the rest of me. Greg and Olivia will be there. What about Clive? He might, out of respect, and for the kids' sake. But I won't know, will I?

Our children—Clive's and my children—are older than Ashley. He hated any reminder of that. When he asked for a divorce, he told me that she was very young.

"How young?"

"Twenty-two."

I burst out laughing. "My God, and you're fifty! Why marry her? You could adopt her instead. She could be a little sister for Greg and Olivia."

"Don't be ridiculous."

"Yeah, you're right. You can't have sex with her if you adopt her. It would be incest, wouldn't it? And that's illegal." I couldn't stop laughing. Tears ran down my cheeks.

"You don't need to get hysterical," He turned red, then white, then he walked out. The next I heard from him was a lawyer's letter.

Everything was done as the law prescribed. My lawyer told me what I was entitled to, and I got it. Clive bought my share of the house. He lives there now with Ashley.

But it's still my house. I don't give a damn whose name is on the deed; it's my house and always will be. Clive must know that. Together we designed it, paid for it, raised our family in it. I know every inch of that house, just like I know every inch of Clive. Hair, eyes, mouth, skin, arms, legs, chest, belly, penis, even those pasty white buttocks. I don't care if we are divorced. I don't care whether he and Ashley have a marriage certificate. He's still my husband.

"With my body I thee worship ..." Of all the words in the marriage service, I treasured those the most. And they were true. With his eyes, his hands, his tongue, Clive's body worshipped me. And he adored my breasts, my lovely, smooth conical breasts with their soft pink nipples.

"After a valiant battle with cancer, Phyllis Moore passed away ..." That's what my obituary will say. I wonder how many people know the horror of that battle. The knife, the waiting; the radiation, the waiting; the chemotherapy, the waiting. I was valiant through all that. What defeated me was the look on Clive's face when he saw the scar where my left breast used to be. His eyes were averted while his mouth recited the words, "It's you I love, not your body parts."

Oh, sure! How often did we make love after that? He tried exactly once. I felt his flesh shrink when his fingers brushed my scar.

I give Clive credit for one thing: he thought the cancer was gone. So did I. Two years after the mastectomy, my X-rays, blood tests and scans all came back clear. Nothing remained but the scar, or so we believed. I'm sure that my husband of twenty-eight years would not knowingly have divorced a dying woman. The final decree came just before I learned that cancer was creeping through my bones. Two final decrees in one month.

After the divorce, my women friends rallied around. Monique, my friend since high school, took me under her wing. She'd been dumped ten years ago, so she considered herself an expert on how to cope. "You need cheering up," she said. "We're going to a nice restaurant for lunch."

The place she took me to was chic and expensive: upholstered chairs, linen napery, a waiter with a towel over his arm. On the table was a single long-stemmed pink rose in a slender vase. The vase was half filled with water. When I bent my head to smell the rose, I saw that it was plastic.

"Look at that," I said. "They've stuck a plastic flower in water. Isn't that the dumbest thing to do?"

Monique rolled her eyes. "It's just to give a natural effect."

"At least I hope the food is real." I was feeling nasty. Why had I let Monique bring me here? For the first time I realized how much I disliked everything about her: her rouged cheeks, polished fingernails, and dyed brown hair. I hated Monique because I was going to die, and she wasn't. That knowledge put a gulf between us as wide as the St. Lawrence. I could have told Monique that there are only two kinds of people in the world: the living and the dying. She didn't know about the metastasis.

"Phyllis, you need counselling. You've got to get rid of all that resentment you carry around inside."

"Uh-huh." I nibbled a tiny cube of plastic cheese.

"You've got to move on. The rest of your life lies ahead. Make a plan for what you're going to do next. Put Clive behind you. There's more to life than being married. Look to the future."

"Monique, why does everything you say sound like a clipping from Ann Landers?"

She looked hurt. "I'm just trying to help."

"I'll be fine," I said. "I don't need any help."

"But what are you going to do?"

"I'll manage."

What was I going to do? I needed no plan. My days were fully occupied with Ashley. With following Ashley, that is. No way I would tell Monique how I had observed Ashley's schedules, learned the route she took to work, waited at the corners of side streets for her red Neon to go by. Monique would think I was crazy if she knew how I loitered in front of shops across the street from the beauty salon where Ashley worked, pretending to window shop in order to catch glimpses of her as she styled women's hair. Clipping, blowing, curling. She chatted with her clients. She smiled. She laughed.

Most days, Ashley did her shopping on her way home. When she stopped at the liquor store, I pulled up in the parking lot and watched from my car as she went through the checkout with a bottle of wine and occasionally scotch or brandy. Sometimes she went to the drugstore, and I went there too, lingering in the next aisle while she picked up lipstick, toothpaste, cough syrup, tampons (so at least she wasn't pregnant). At the supermarket I followed her with my shopping cart, keeping a few customers between us, while she chose steaks, mushrooms, green grapes, rye bread—all of which proved that Clive's taste in food had not changed.

Even before the night I watched them make love, I had learned a lot about Clive and Ashley's life together. But that was the night I knew it had to stop.

I sip my camomile tea, drift off to sleep, and enter my usual dream. It's an underwater dream. I'm at the bottom of a lake, lying upon soft ripples of sand, lulled by the murmur of moving water as waves roll my body gently back and forth. I feel my flesh loosen from my bones. Soon it will all break away, and I'll be free.

On our twentieth anniversary, Clive gave me a necklace: a star sapphire flanked by four strands of matching pearls. It came in a blue velvet box.

Now, for the first time in years, I take the box from my dresser drawer. The lid snaps open, and there lies my necklace on a bed of quilted satin. I take it from the box and put it on. The sapphire rests in the hollow of my throat. I turn my head from side to side to follow the gleam of the fugitive star.

Ashley's eyes are sapphire blue. My necklace would suit her beauty. But I do not intend her to have it. It's the bait. I return the necklace to its box.

Clive's phone number is unlisted. He had it changed months ago to avoid my phone calls. I used to phone nearly every day, just to listen to his voice, or hers, depending on who answered. That's what I did before I started following Ashley. I had no difficulty getting the new number from a mutual friend, but I've never used it until now.

I press the buttons, take a deep breath, and wait for Ashley to pick up the receiver. She must answer. I don't want to talk to a machine. Ring. Ring. Ring. I'm sweating, and my hand trembles. Why doesn't she answer? The beauty shop is closed on Mondays, and it's too early for her to have gone out. Ring. Ring. Then I hear her voice.

"Hello."

"This is Phyllis."

"Oh."

"I've been wanting to call you for some time, but of course it's difficult."

"I heard you were ill. I'm sorry."

"I have health problems. But that's not what I'm calling about."

Silence on the line. She waits for me to explain.

"I have a necklace," I say, "that belonged to Clive's mother. Four strands of pearls with a star sapphire at the centre. It's no longer a jewel that I feel comfortable wearing. If you would like it, I feel that you are the person who should have it."

She lets out her breath. "Clive never mentioned ..."

"I don't suppose he would. Clive is too much a gentleman to have asked me to return it. But if you're uncomfortable with the idea ..."

"Oh, no! It sounds beautiful." So now the little mouse is sniffing the cheese.

"Then can you come over this morning to get it? Ten o'clock, say? I have a medical appointment later, and I'd really like to get this done and over with."

It's already nine in the morning. I don't want to give her time to phone Clive at his office, although it doesn't matter. Even if she did phone him, Clive would be too tactful to tell her that the necklace had been my anniversary gift from him. He might wonder why I don't just sell it or give it to Olivia if I don't want to keep it. But, knowing Clive, I think he would go along with my story so that Ashley could have the necklace—unless he suspected a trap.

Ashley doesn't hesitate. "I've just had a shower. I'll be over as soon as I'm dressed. That should be a few minutes after ten."

So that's what took her so long to get to the phone. Taking a shower. The water pressure is not too good in the ensuite. I wonder whether she showers in the main bathroom instead, as I used to do.

I get everything ready. The necklace, nestled in its blue velvet box, rests on my coffee table. I arrange cookies on a plate, take out my best china cups and saucers, set everything on a silver tray. If I still had a garden, I could decorate the tray with a few late chrysanthemums; but my garden is another thing I've lost.

I sharpen the blades of my kitchen scissors. Then I count out the sleeping pills that I've been saving for so long: twenty for Ashley and twenty for me. Will those be enough? Well, they have to be. I put them back into the bottle and go into the bedroom to put on my wig.

Ashley rings from the lobby, and I press the button to let her in. I can time practically to the second how long it will take her to wait for the elevator, reach the twelfth floor, come along the hall and knock at my door.

While I wait, I can hardly breathe for nervousness. I wish I could talk to Olivia about the way I feel. When it's over, will she understand? Greg won't, but then he never tries. Clive will understand; I intend to make sure of that.

At Ashley's knock, I open the door. Ashley is petite, half a head shorter than I am. Beside her, I feel tall and clumsy. When she turns her head, her hair swings like a model's in a shampoo commercial. Poker-straight hair, side-parted and held back with a single gold clip. I wonder whether she irons her hair. That's what I did in the 1970s, when I was her age.

With a smile, I hang up her jacket, try to put her at ease. It's obvious that she doesn't want to meet my eye. But between avoiding my wig and my bosom, her eyes have nowhere to rest. After jittering around the room, they settle on the coffee table and the blue velvet box.

"Won't you sit down," I motion her toward an uphol-stered chair. She sits awkwardly, as if unsure what to do with her knees. "A cup of tea? Or would you rather have coffee?"

"I won't have anything, thank you."

"But you must."

What choice does she have but to accept my hospitality? There on the coffee table sits the blue velvet box, almost within her grasp. She can't just pick it up and leave, though that's obviously what she would like to do.

"Tea would be nice."

I would prefer her to have said coffee. But if I make Earl Grey extra strong, she won't notice anything unusual. And even if she does, she won't say anything—not with that blue velvet box sitting there. Anyway, who knows what sleeping pills taste like dissolved in tea?

I excuse myself, leaving her staring at the blue velvet box. In the kitchen I make two pots of tea, dumping twenty sleeping pills into the teapot with the long, curved spout. I stir briskly to make sure that they dissolve, then carry both teapots into the living room and set them down on the tray.

"Regular or decaffeinated?" I ask.

"Oh, it doesn't matter."

"I'll give you regular, then. You're too young to worry about caffeine."

She doesn't object. I fill her cup with tea from the pot with the long, curved spout, and mine from the other.

"Milk and sugar?" I ask.

"Both. Lots of sugar."

I'm happy to oblige.

A tiny frown appears between her perfect eyebrows as she drinks the tea, but she says nothing. I wait until her cup is empty before opening the box. Her eyes widen when she sees my necklace resting on the white satin lining, the pearls and the sapphire shimmering with cold fire.

"It's so beautiful!" Her right hand reaches forward timidly, then stops in mid-air.

"Go ahead," I say. "Try it on."

She picks up the necklace, fumbles with the clasp. "I can't get this undone."

"It's a special clasp, impossible to open accidentally. I'll help you."

I take the necklace from her, and she turns partly around, lifting her long, honey-coloured hair out of the way. What a soft, tender, childlike neck she has! I secure the clasp.

"There's a mirror in the hall, so you can see how it looks on you."

Ashley rises a couple of inches, then sinks back in her chair. "I feel dizzy," she says, and looks at me with a puzzled expression. "Dizzy." In five minutes, she's out cold.

She sleeps like a baby—so cuddly and soft she ought to be hugging a teddy bear. Sweet. That's how Clive first described her: "I don't expect you to like her, but she's a sweet girl."

I had answered: "Whether or not I like her is scarcely the issue, since I don't expect ever to meet her."

But here she is, sprawled unconscious on an armchair in my living room, with my twentieth anniversary necklace around her lovely neck. The skin of her throat is soft and milky, as white as pearls. I stand over her, pick up a strand of her hair and let it slide like a skein of silk through my fingers.

Does Clive do this? Does he tell her that her hair is like silk? Then I remember how her curtain of hair hid Clive's face the night I watched through the window, and my rage returns. But it's cold rage now. Who was it that said, "Revenge is a dish best served cold?"

I return to my seat, finish my harmless cup of tea, eat a shortbread and then a macaroon. The sun has risen over the building across the street. Sunlight floods my living room. Sunlight in Ashley's hair spins flax into gold. She is on display for me, like a princess doll in a shop window. Rapunzel, Rapunzel, let down your hair!

She is still breathing when I leave the room, still breathing when I return from the kitchen with the scissors in my hand. I start to cut, hacking as close to the roots as I can. Pale gold all the way. Natural blond hair was nature's gift to Ashley. Now nature can have it back.

As I sever each lock, I lay it carefully on the coffee table, making sure that all strands run the same way. Such beautiful hair, so long and fine. I could have a wig made from it. Now that's an idea! I laugh to think of Clive's reaction if he saw me in a wig made of Ashley's hair. Snip. Snip. I keep on cutting.

Poor Ashley. She looks like a waif with her hair hacked off. Nothing left but ragged tufts on a scalp nearly as bald as mine.

Her breathing has stopped. I lower my head to her chest, but hear nothing. My cheek rests upon her bosom. What full breasts she has for so slender a girl! I undo the buttons of her blouse, pull down the left strap of Ashley's brassiere. Her breast is smooth and conical, with a pink nipple.

I squeeze the nipple between my fingertips and gently pull it between the open blades of my kitchen scissors.

I go into the kitchen to rinse the stickiness off my fingers. I dry my hands on a paper towel and return to prepare the jewellery box. After I have wrapped the box in brown paper and written Clive's address on the mailing label, I take a bath—a long, relaxing bath, with lavender salts in the water. I rub my body with lotion. My scar no longer troubles me.

Now I must choose the right thing to wear. Perhaps my silk suit is not appropriate for a trip to the post office, but this is a special occasion. I'll take my sleeping pills as soon as I get back.

Too bad I won't be around when Clive opens the blue velvet box. I'd love to see his face when he finds Ashley's golden hair coiled on the white satin lining, with her pink nipple resting on top like the jewel in her crown.

A Neighbourly Thing To Do

The woman next door was taking a long time to die.

Christine had not gone to see her. At first she had meant to, but always put it off. And the longer she put it off, the harder it was to go. She had no excuses.

"Don't you think you should?" Mac said over Sunday breakfast. "They've been good neighbours."

"Why don't you go, then?"

"You're the woman," he said, and spread marmalade on his toast.

Christine shrugged, knowing what he meant. "I want to remember her the way she was, not yellow and shrunk, the way they get."

"That makes it easy for you." She knew that Mac meant it as a criticism. Easy for Christine. Not for Frances, the woman who had already spent six months dying in the house next door.

Mac got up from the table and pushed in his chair. "Think about it. We've got some nice daffodils in the garden. You could take her a bunch."

Mac had to go down to the store. He always did the books on Sunday mornings, because the store was closed and there was no one about to disturb him. The store was a drugstore, but Mac wasn't a pharmacist. He should have been, but there hadn't been a college of pharmacy in the country that would accept him, not with his high school grades. He had repeated some entrance subjects a couple of times, trying to improve his marks. Mac was no quitter. Eventually his father had to tell him to give up: "You can hire a pharmacist to work for you if you want to keep the store."

Mac did want to keep it. It was the oldest drugstore in Clayton. His grandfather had founded it: "Mackenzie's Family Pharmacy." Mac's father had become a pharmacist and taken it over. Mac grew up expecting to do the same. As a boy he took for granted that someday his framed diploma would hang on the dispensary wall along with his father's and grandfather's. To be Ross Mackenzie, PhmB, was the height of his ambition.

If Mac had had a lofty goal, such as to be Prime Minister or CEO of the Royal Bank, he would have felt less shame at failure. It galled him not to have a degree. When he walked down the street he couldn't help feeling that people pointed at him and whispered, "He's not really a pharmacist. Not smart enough." He knew that the idea was ridiculous, that he was respected as a businessman. People brought their prescriptions to be filled at his dispensary. But not by him. It was the man he employed who had the PhmB.

When he asked Christine to marry him, he had confessed it almost as if he were confiding a shameful secret, like illegitimacy or a family history of madness. But Christine hadn't cared. She had a calm way of accepting things, even things that bothered him a lot.

Such as the woman next door. It wasn't Frances herself that bothered him, but the fact that she lay there dying while he went on with his ordinary life. She had been beautiful last spring—one year ago. Tall, lithe, with russet hair, green eyes, and pale skin covered with soft freckles. That's how he would like to remember her. He shouldn't blame Christine for feeling the same.

Christine did not visit Frances, but a couple of times a week she saw Frances' husband. He was a tall man with broad shoulders, curly black hair and tender brown eyes. He always arrived home from work at ten to six, in time to take over from the nurse who looked after his wife during the day. On the weekends he took care of her himself. His name was Gord. He was about forty years old, the same as Christine.

Whenever she saw him, Christine asked about Frances. She gave him messages for her. "Please tell Frances that I'm thinking about her," which was true. Gord always thanked her and went into the house. He had a tired walk. By the end of winter, he began to stoop.

After Mac had left for the drugstore, Christine cleaned up the kitchen. When the counters were wiped and the sink scrubbed, she opened the back door to take out the garbage. For her it was an ordinary Sunday morning, until she felt the sunshine on her face and the warm breeze on her skin and saw the yellow daffodils at the bottom of the garden. She put the garbage in the trash can and looked again. The daffodils nodded their heads to her. She crossed the grass, bent amongst them, and found herself snapping their crisp stalks at the base. When she straightened her back, her hands were full with daffodils, her fingers sticky with their juice, and her bare arms dusted with a shower of gold.

I'll take them to Frances, she thought. Mac was right. She would take them to Frances now, before any second thoughts weakened her resolve. Christine carried the daffodils like a chalice to the house next door and rang the doorbell.

Gord opened the door. He needed a shave, and he looked tired. Christine thrust the flowers towards him, thinking as she did that she should not have come. Or at least she should have phoned first, and she definitely should have brought the daffodils in a vase.

He smiled at her, a wistful, uncertain smile. In his eyes she saw loneliness and also a need that clutched at her own insides. The daffodil heads bobbed up and down. Christine's hands were trembling as Gord took the flowers from her. His fingers were warm.

"Frances is asleep," he told her. "Or I'm sure she'd love to see you." He opened the door wider and motioned Christine to step into the hall. "She was awake all night." He didn't need to say that he was too.

"I should have put the flowers in a vase," she said. "I'm sorry."

"That doesn't matter. We have lots." He looked down at the bunch of daffodils in his hands. "Maybe you'll help me choose which one, sort of arrange the flowers so they'll look nice."

Christine could have said that daffodils don't need to be arranged. All you have to do is stick them in water. If she had said that, it would not have been necessary to go into the kitchen with him.

But here she was, standing in the middle of a kitchen floor that was sticky under the soles of her shoes, facing a counter stacked with dirty dishes and a sink filled with pans. "Sorry for you to see this mess," he said. "I should have put them in the dishwasher." He smiled helplessly and shrugged. "If I'd known you were coming …"

"You'd have baked a cake?" They shared a smile.

"Really," she said, "the mess doesn't bother me. Just show me where you keep your vases."

He brought out two and set them on the kitchen table, then brought out two more, and two more after that. Green glass, clear glass, cut crystal, porcelain, pottery. "Enough," she said. "Any one of these is fine."

He wanted her to make a choice, and it should have been easy. It would have been easy if she hadn't been alone with him, if his eyes hadn't been tired and his smile helpless and his broad shoulders stooped. "This one." She picked up the green glass vase and gave it to him. He had bony fingers with black hairs on them, and there were black hairs on his wrists. He had to move a saucepan out of the way to get the top of the vase under the faucet. She watched the stream of water fill the vase to the top. "That's too much," she said. "It will overflow when you put the flowers in."

She shouldn't have smiled as she took the vase from his hands and poured the excess water into the sink. They were alone in the kitchen. His sick wife was asleep upstairs. Christine wasn't planning anything. She meant to put the daffodils into the vase and go home. But his eyes were tired and so sad.

The minute she set down the vase and took his hand, she knew what would happen next.

His touch was electric, and his mouth was lightning and soft rain all at once. She pressed her body to his body. He leaned his face into her neck, and she reached down to touch the crotch of his jeans, to feel the pulse and heat centred there. This was real to her; real and yet deeply strange.

Afterwards they rolled apart and lay not facing one another. The floor was dirty, and Frances was asleep upstairs. Christine got up, put on her panties, smoothed her skirt over her hips. Gord looked at her with a kind of stunned dis-belief. "I didn't mean for that to happen," he said.

"No. Neither did I."

She put the daffodils into the vase without looking at him, wanting only to get back to her own kitchen where the floor was clean.

"I went next door to visit Frances," she said to Mac as they ate lunch. "I took her some daffodils, as you suggested. She was asleep, so I didn't see her. Gord said that he'd give her the flowers when she woke up."

"Good," said Mac. "It was a neighbourly thing to do."

Christine did not go next door again. She saw Gord as often as before, coming home from work or working in his yard. They spoke politely to each other. He always looked tired. She saw that he was losing weight.

When Frances finally died, Christine and Mac went to the funeral. Soon after that, a For Sale sign appeared on Gord's lawn.

Christine hoped that the house wouldn't take a long time to sell.

Out! Out!

Last night Evelyn dreamed she was drowning. It was a dream she had had many times before. The pounding in her ears. The sensation that her lungs were about to burst. The refusal of her body to obey her mind's instructions. The weight that dragged her down. She awoke with a gasp, sweating in terror.

The dream lingered throughout the day. Once she had to pause in the midst of teaching a lesson to gulp for air, and even after the last class of students had filed out of the classroom the feeling stayed. It did not interfere with carrying out her normal routine. She tidied her desk. She picked up a piece of chalk in the usual way and wrote the usual notices in the upper right hand corner of the blackboard. On May 17, 12C would be tested on *Macbeth*. 11D had an essay due

May 11. "PLO" she wrote in big letters, directing the cleaners to Please Leave On. As she laid the chalk in the chalk trough, it occurred to Evelyn that the letters also stood for "Palestine Liberation Organization."

How many students would study for the test or write the essay? Maybe one out of five. A strike was coming, and the kids knew it. With luck, everyone in 12C and 11D would get credit for the year without doing another lick of work.

With a sigh, she surveyed the empty classroom. Six rows of desks, eight in each row. For thirty years she had faced the occupants of those desks. Girls with poodle skirts, miniskirts, hot pants, blue jeans, and belly-baring tights. Boys with crew cuts, long hair, dreadlocks, scalp locks, shaved heads, green hair in spikes. Hormone-ridden adolescents with blank faces. How interchangeable they all seemed!

Many of her students were the offspring of the first ones she had taught. Soon their grandchildren would occupy the same seats.

Evelyn had never wanted to be a teacher. It was books she loved, not kids. She had backed into this career as she had backed into everything in her life. But what else could you do when you'd flunked out of grad school?

She'd backed into marriage—also because of books. Paperbacks 25¢. Hard covers at various prices. You never knew what you'd find at Henry Frizzell's used bookstore on Barton Street. She went there on a book hunt every couple of months, usually on a Wednesday after school, because the shop wasn't busy then and Henry Frizzell had time to help her search.

She went to Henry's store for books, not sex. But at the ripe and anxious age of forty, she'd backed into that too.

Virginia Woolf had caused it all. Henry was positive that he had a copy of *The Waves* somewhere on his dusty shelves. She searched. He searched. They searched together for an hour after he had locked the door and hung the CLOSED sign in the window. At last, amongst the travel books, he found it.

"This calls for a celebration," he said. "I'll make coffee."

Evelyn glanced at her wristwatch. She hadn't yet marked 9c's test on Greek myths, the results promised back tomorrow.

"I'm not sure that I have time."

"There's always time for coffee." He opened the door to his cramped office at the back of the store. Through the open doorway she watched him pull two chipped mugs from a dusty shelf. After shoving a stack of National Geographic magazines out of the way, he set the mugs on his desk. One displayed a leaping tiger with the motto: Hamilton Tiger Cats 1972 Grey Cup Champions. The other had a picture of Santa Claus.

"Sit down while I boil the water. This just takes a minute."

She entered the office but remained standing while he plugged in the kettle.

"Take a seat," he insisted, and gave a half spin to the swivel chair in front of his desk so that it faced the ancient leather sofa. Might as well, she thought.

The coffee was lousy—"No Name" instant with soluble enzymes instead of cream. She sat stiffly on the swivel chair, sipping from the Santa Claus mug while Henry positioned himself on the sofa. He had a face that reminded her of old leather, dry and cracked. His hair was brown mixed with grey. His eyes were dark and opaque, like chocolate.

"What do you do for a living?" As he leaned intimately toward her, the sofa creaked.

From nervousness she told him more than the question required, including the story of her expulsion from grad school Eden to the hell of teachers' college.

"You don't wear a wedding ring," he observed.

"I'm not married."

"Good reason."

The following Wednesday she returned. This time she sat beside him on the sofa. When he put his arm around her, she did not retreat, although the feeling that his touch aroused was more curiosity than desire. He shifted his body closer, kissed her neck, ears, cheeks and mouth. When he touched her breast, shivers ran through her. His stroking hand moved further down.

There could be no doubt what he had in mind. Should she tell him that she was a virgin? A virgin at forty! He might laugh. Worse still, he might stop.

Afterwards, when he pulled up his zipper and she untangled her pantyhose, Evelyn decided that the experience had been more or less satisfactory, despite the sofa's broken springs.

Sex on Wednesdays became as much a part of Evelyn's routine as her standing appointment to get her hair done every Friday. They had made love weekly for two months when one evening, just as they finished, the telephone rang.

"Better get that." Extricating himself from between Evelyn's legs, he shuffled to the desk and picked up the handset. She could not hear the caller's voice.

"Milk. Okay, Ida. Anything else?" He pulled up his zipper and winked at Evelyn, shrugging one shoulder as if to say: "You know how it is."

"Butter, orange juice, cat food. No, I won't forget. I'm writing it down." He wasn't.

"You didn't tell me you were married," said Evelyn as she tucked in her blouse.

"Oh, didn't I?" He turned his chocolate gaze toward her. "I thought I had."

Although the news was a surprise, she hadn't minded that he was married. It was, in fact, an advantage. Sex at 5:30, when the bookshop closed, meant that she could drive home after the rush hour and still finish supper by 7:30, leaving the evening clear to work on lesson plans.

She suspected that sex with Henry wasn't great. About C+ if she had to assign a mark. But then, Evelyn had had nothing with which to compare it.

The wall clock in her classroom said 3:15. Evelyn got to her feet and picked up her daybook and two fat bundles of test papers held together with elastic bands. She opened her briefcase. (Scuffed, brown leather with sturdy straps, it had served her since graduate school more than thirty years ago). She stuffed in the test papers, together with her teaching copy of *Macbeth*.

"Tomorrow and tomorrow and tomorrow / Creeps in this petty pace from day to day ..." she muttered as she closed the classroom door behind her.

Green lockers lined the hall, locker after locker after locker for the length of a city block, interrupted only by doors to classrooms, and halfway to the staircase, a drinking fountain. Thirty years ago, water had spurted from it like a virgin spring. Clogged pipes now slowed it to a trickle. She stopped anyway, pressed the button to coax out a feeble stream. At the bottom of the basin lay a wad of chewing gum and a sodden tissue. Evelyn changed her mind.

In the Staff Room, Evelyn's colleagues clustered around tables or huddled on the sofas that lined the walls, waiting for the hands of the wall clock to reach 3:45. At the table closest to the windows, the auto mechanics teacher and the Head of Mathematics played their usual Friday chess game. Today it did not appear to absorb them, for after every move both players glanced at the clock. Madame Simone, who taught French, was knitting a pale green sweater while her eyes followed the second hand as it slowly swept the dial.

As always, the teachers reminded Evelyn of a flock of sheep waiting to be let out of their pen.

"Pen." An interesting word. "Pent up" must have come from the same root. As Evelyn poured a cup of pseudo-coffee from the vending machine, she considered its various meanings. The sheepfold kind of pen. The pen that's mightier than the sword. The pen that's short for "penitentiary." Yes, that fit. At 3:30 on Friday afternoons, the teachers always looked like prisoners waiting to be released. But today the atmosphere was full of a unique, unusual tension. There had never been a strike before.

Evelyn sat down at the only table that had a free chair. On her left was steadfast Miss Trotter, the history teacher, who had never missed a day in forty years. On Evelyn's right was Shelley Grubb, the union boss, whose first name was really Beulah. Across the table the youngest member of staff, Tim Fergus, who taught Special Education, slumped despondently.

"When I started teaching ..." Miss Trotter, her jowls quivering, was making a speech, "I had fifty in my classroom." She looked at her companions searchingly, as if to make sure they knew how many fifty was. "We had desks in the aisles, desks beside the windows, desks along the side wall blocking off the blackboard. Fifty students in every class. I had one spare each week. And I never complained."

Ms. Grubb glowered. "Slave labour. You didn't have to take that."

"It was my duty," said Miss Trotter. Her triple chin joined the jowls, all trembling in unison.

"Bullshit," said Ms. Grubb. "Your duty was to the other teachers. You needed a union."

Tim, who did not seem to be listening, sighed. "Today the boys climbed out the window and ran away. After that, the girls said there wasn't any point in me teaching the lesson because I'd have to teach it all over again when the boys came back."

"I hope you taught it anyway," said Miss Trotter.

"No, the girls were right."

"What do you normally teach the students in Special Ed?" Evelyn asked.

"Nothing. The teaching goals are literacy, numeracy and good citizenship. But the kids don't want to learn."

"If you cannot inspire a love of learning," said Miss Trotter sternly, "you don't belong in teaching."

Tim shrugged. "I have twenty-thousand dollars in student loans to pay off. What would you have me do? Change my name and skip town?"

Evelyn set down her Styrofoam cup. She wanted to shout: "Yes! Save yourself before it's too late!" But she didn't dare. The others would think she was having a nervous breakdown. It would be quite out of character for Mrs. Evelyn Frizzell to give such advice. After all, she was a senior teacher—a model of responsibility.

Always a model of responsibility. Probably that explained why she had let Henry in when he appeared at the door of her condominium with two suitcases.

"Ida knows about us. She's thrown me out."

"How did she find out?"

"Lipstick on my collar."

Evelyn gaped. The triteness, the cheapness of it made

her furious. Already she regretted the whole thing. It was humiliating to be caught in so pointless, so accidental a relationship. She refused to call it a love affair, for they never even took off their clothes.

"You can't stay here. I'm a teacher. You'll get me fired."

"I have nowhere to go."

She should have shut the door, not stood wavering.

"Just till you find an apartment," she said.

There were advantages. Sex was better in bed, with clean sheets and good firm springs. Evelyn's visits to the bookstore ceased.

From time to time, when Henry's buying expeditions yielded books that Evelyn would enjoy, he brought a few home. Virginia Woolf. E. M. Forster. Evelyn Waugh. Henry was good about that.

Then one day he brought home the bookshop's entire inventory, transported it to Evelyn's apartment in a Rent-All Truck while she was at school.

No advance warning. She opened the door and there they were, covering the front hall, living room and dining room and kitchen floors. Forty-seven cartons of books.

"Good God! Where did these come from?"

"Not enough business on Barton Street. I couldn't pay the rent. Anyway, I can work just as well from here."

"Turn my condo into a bookshop?"

His chocolate eyes gleamed as he handed her a business card.

She read aloud: "*F. W. Frizzell. Rare and Out of Print Books. By appointment only.*" At the bottom of the card were her address and telephone number.

"No!" She took a deep breath. "I don't think so."

"I got rid of the junk. This is the good stuff."

"No."

Henry sighed and ran his hand through his greying hair. He looked around the room, and Evelyn recognized the kind of look he was giving her place, the kind of assessment.

"There's plenty of room for more bookcases. One in the hall, two in the living room, two in the dining room if we move the buffet. And we can squeeze one into the bedroom."

"No."

"It's not as if I'd be in your way." He ran his fingers through his hair again. "You never get home till after four o'clock."

"No."

"Come on. Give me a break." His chocolate eyes pleaded.

"I already did. You've been living here rent-free for a year."

"Evelyn, I want to contribute. We'll get married. My divorce will be final in a week."

"I don't want to get married."

"If I make an honest woman of you, you won't have to worry about your job."

"Don't be daft."

But his idea was not daft. People were talking, and she knew it. In a discreet interview, the Principal had informed her about parents' complaints to members of the Board of Education. The unfairness of it irked her, but it was pointless to deny the truth. Although the rest of the world could live in sin, teachers were expected to exemplify all virtues.

Evelyn's head was starting to pound. She didn't want to think about it any more. If she couldn't get rid of Henry and his books, marriage was the only way out.

Within a month they were married.

For five years she endured the books, and they weren't the worst of it. Life with Henry meant gobs of toothpaste in her bathroom sink, the scurf of whiskers clinging to the porcelain after he shaved, the toilet seat left up, the dirty socks on the bedroom floor. She felt herself debased. When, oh when, would she be able to regain her territory?

Henry was indignant at her criticism.

"Ida never complained."

"But she kicked you out."

"She kicked me out because of you."

Evelyn sighed. "So I'm responsible? Yes, I suppose I am."

The staff room conversation had shifted.

"If there's a strike," Tim asked, "will we have to walk on a picket line?"

"Of course," said Ms. Grubb.

"I will not," said Miss Trotter, her jowls quivering. "Nor will I abandon my students. To do so would be a violation of every principle I cherish."

"What will you do, then?" Evelyn asked, feeling a thrill of admiration for the old warhorse.

"I shall battle through the picket line, enter the school, and sit in my classroom ready to teach."

"Then, when the strike ends," said Ms. Grubb grimly, "and you walk into this staff room, no one will speak to you. You will be shunned." With those words she rose to her feet and stalked off.

Miss Trotter looked at Tim, then at Evelyn. Neither offered support. After a minute Evelyn said, "You could retire."

Miss Trotter's response set off further vibrations of jowls and triple chin. "Evelyn, I could have retired on full pension eight years ago, but would not leave the students of Fairview Collegiate to … to …"

To what? To whom? To the likes of Shelley Grubb, Miss Trotter probably meant.

The hands of the clock moved to 3:45. With a scraping of chairs, everyone got up.

"Well, maybe I'll see you guys Monday," Tim said as he unfolded himself from his chair. "Or maybe I won't."

Maybe. The deadline was midnight tonight. If negotiations failed, the teachers would be out. If a contract were reached, life at Fairview would go on as usual.

Evelyn and Miss Trotter were the only teachers left in the staff room. Neither made any move to get up.

"What will you do, Evelyn?" Miss Trotter asked.

"Maybe I should climb out the window like the boys in Special Ed." Evelyn looked towards the staff room window. Freedom was so close.

She'd almost gained it once, nine years ago, when Henry had died. Death by books. He had purchased a complete set of the Encyclopedia Britannica, Ninth Edition, at an estate sale held in the basement of St. Ignatius Church. After carrying the last of six cartons up the stairs and out to the parking lot, he had keeled over.

The doctor had made Evelyn sit down to receive the news: Henry dead of a massive heart attack. "You're in shock," he had said. Evelyn, her whole body shaking (for she was indeed in shock) suppressed the joyful shout that forced its way from deep within. Henry gone! Her big mistake so neatly erased!

She had put his clothes out with the garbage and sold the bookcases and the books—except for a few that she liked— to one of Henry's competitors. That's when she should have broken free, all the way free.

Evelyn stood up, lifting her briefcase from the floor beside her chair. The weight of it made her sag. "Well, goodbye."

Miss Trotter raised her eyes to Evelyn's. Her lips quivered, as if there were something she wanted to tell Evelyn. The moment passed.

"Goodbye," said Miss Trotter.

Evelyn carried her briefcase across the room, stopped at the door and looked back. Miss Trotter was taking her coat from the rack.

"Miss Trotter!"

Miss Trotter turned around.

Evelyn took a deep breath. "I won't be back."

Miss Trotter stood still. She pulled her scarf from the sleeve of her coat and knotted it about her neck. "A wise decision." She nodded her head so slowly that the jowls did not move. "Have a good life."

As Evelyn walked to the parking lot, excitement welled up inside like a bubble ready to burst. Her heart pounded as she placed the briefcase on the passenger's seat, turned on the ignition, and drove away.

Evelyn parked in the lay-by near the High Level Bridge and got out of the car, carrying her briefcase. She walked to the middle of the bridge, where she stopped, leaned over the concrete parapet, and stared down at the brown water ninety feet below.

Over the years, there had been days of despair when Evelyn had considered jumping from this bridge. "To die, to sleep— / To sleep—perchance to dream." Her nightmare again—death by water. The horror of drowning, drowning forever through all eternity. She took a deep breath to banish the thought.

Far below, barely beneath the water's surface, clusters of orange and brown carp rolled and swirled. They looked like monstrous goldfish as they circled in the still water, going nowhere. Not that different from a flock of sheep. She laughed. Not that different from a staff room full of teachers.

What if one fish broke away? What if it said to itself: "To hell with this! Why should I waste my life swimming in circles between a sandbar and a marsh? I'll break away! I'll spread my fins and go where no carp has gone before."

Evelyn smiled as she lifted her briefcase over the parapet. She gripped its sturdy handle and held it at arm's length as far out as she could, then let go. Down, down it fell. She saw the splash. The carp dispersed, their backs breaking the surface as they fled.

She watched the briefcase drift about, sagging at one end like a listing ship until it took the final plunge.

The carp came back and resumed their circling. Evelyn shouted to them, "Fish, get those test papers marked by Monday. The office needs the results by nine o'clock."

Evelyn raised her face to the sky and took a great gulp of fresh air. Oxygen. She felt like singing as she walked away.

The War Guest

Peggy kneels on the living room carpet, unpacking the last of the cartons that she brought from the house. She has left this one until the end because she doesn't know what to do with its contents. Her condo is short of storage space. Where is she going to put eight scrapbooks bulging with greeting cards, birth notices, baptismal certificates, school report cards, wedding announcements and ration cards?

She wasn't the one who had collected this stuff. That was Mother. But Peggy is heir to it. There are two scrapbooks devoted to Mother and Father, two to Peggy, and two each to her brothers. Peggy's scrapbooks cover her life from birth until marriage. The last item pasted to the last page is a wedding invitation. After Peggy's marriage, Mother probably expected her to start her own scrapbooks. She never did. What was the point?

Her two brothers didn't want their scrapbooks. "You hold on to them," they told Peggy. Throwing them out was not contemplated.

Mother had used children's scribblers for the scrapbooks. Each has a picture of Snow White dancing with the Seven Dwarfs on its front cover, with a set of arithmetical tables on its back. When Peggy was a child, scribblers always had arithmetical tables on the back, even when the front looked like a comic book. Presumably this was to promote a healthy balance of work and play.

Eight identical scrapbooks. Mother must have bought them all at the same time, divining long ago how she would fill them through the years.

Peggy picks up the two that have her name on the cover and carries them to an armchair by the window to catch the afternoon light. She opens the first.

The pages are yellow and brittle—wartime paper. But the things pasted to them are in pretty good shape. Peggy's birth announcement is on page one—embossed lettering on white card: "John and Eleanor Lamb announce the birth of Margaret Jane." Margaret—always called Peggy—was the firstborn. Her brothers' less distinguished birth announcements were of the ready-made kind, with a sugary verse and blank spaces for new parents to fill in the vital facts.

Peggy had been born on December 1, 1933. She weighed nine pounds. Friends and relatives obviously rejoiced at her birth; their congratulatory letters and cards fill six pages.

She flips quickly until she reaches the page where her own memories begin. This is where it starts to hurt. To look at these birthday cards, party invitations and school reports feels like pulling the scab off a half-healed wound, the way she used to do when she was seven years old.

Peggy's Grade Two report card is in the scrapbook, its brown paper envelope glued to the page. As she pulls it out, she remembers the long walk home from Earl Kitchener Public School, clutching the report card in her hand. A's in spelling, B's in arithmetic, and always too many "lates." It comes back to her now—all those times she had been sent to the principal's office for being late. She remembers standing on the corner of Dundurn Street and Aberdeen Avenue, terrified of the cars that whizzed by. No crossing guards in those days. She walked to school by herself. And wasn't that strange, come to think of it, that in a world engulfed in war, traffic was the only thing a Canadian child had to fear as she walked alone to and from school?

Earl Kitchener Public School was four blocks north of Orchard Hill, the street where Peggy lived. For her, the school was a boundary marker and its playground a frontier. Neighbourhoods north of Earl Kitchener were out of bounds, for everyone knew that nice people lived in the south part of the city close to the base of the Escarpment and tough people in the north end near the railroad tracks. When you lived halfway between, like Peggy's family, you had to be careful about your choice of friends.

She once received a birthday party invitation from a girl

who lived near the railroad tracks. "You can't go there!" Mother said. Peggy forgets what excuse Mother told her to make, but remembers that she hadn't wanted to go to the party anyway. The birthday girl, who sat in front of her at school, had cooties crawling through her hair.

The next page of the scrapbook has 1940 written at the top. Peggy turns half a dozen pages filled with valentines from classmates whom she has forgotten. Following the valentine cards is a certificate from the Canadian Red Cross, thanking Margaret Lamb for her one-dollar contribution to the War Effort.

The War Effort. When was the last time she heard that phrase? She remembers carrying a can of bacon grease to the movie matinee every Saturday afternoon. The War Effort needed cans of grease, though Peggy had no idea why. She hoped that the brave soldiers overseas had something better than cold bacon grease to eat.

Peggy could not remember a time before The War. Although the fighting was far away, The War was a constant presence in her life. Every Monday she took twenty-five cents to school to buy her War Savings Stamp to put in her War Savings Book. When the book was full, she got a War Savings Certificate. After The War, this certificate would make her rich. But she had not believed in a time after The War any more than in a time before it began.

The War brought three grown-up male cousins for brief visits. They wore bluish-grey uniforms decorated with wings, which meant that they served in the Royal Canadian Air

Force. They stayed for only a few days because they were on leave and their own homes were too far away for them to go there. They gave Peggy nickels, and one of them played Go Fish with her. Mother cried when the cousins were lost, one on a bombing mission, one when his airplane crashed into a mountain in the fog, and the third when he was learning how to fly. No one said that they were dead, just lost. For a long time Peggy had hoped that someone would find her cousins and bring them back.

She had been a lonely child with no close friend until Venetia arrived. That is the best way to put it. Venetia didn't simply come with the neighbourhood, the way other children did. Venetia arrived. There should have been fanfare. There should have been flags.

It was a warm day in the middle of summer. The year was 1941. Peggy was sitting on the porch steps pulling a scab off her knee. The scab was half off when Miss Putnam appeared from around the corner of the street, striding briskly up Orchard Hill. Peggy tried to press the scab back into place so that Miss Putnam wouldn't see what she was doing. But Miss Putnam didn't notice. Her face wore a bright, excited look that Peggy had never seen before. When she turned up the front walk, she asked, "Is your mother at home?"

Of course Mother was at home! Where else would a mother be?

"Yes, Miss Putnam." Peggy stood up. "I'll tell her you're here."

"Actually, my news is for both of you." Miss Putnam smiled. She smiled so hard that Peggy thought her face might crack, for Miss Putnam's stern face seldom smiled. She had been a teacher for years and years, though not at Peggy's school. Peggy had already noticed that teachers got so used to looking strict that they couldn't stop even after they retired.

Mother and Miss Putnam, who lived around the corner on Cottage Avenue, both belonged to the Chedoke Garden Club. Miss Putnam had taught at Lady Byng College, a private school for girls. Mother thought that Miss Putnam was very genteel.

Peggy followed Miss Putnam and Mother into the living room to hear Miss Putnam's news. Peggy remembers her exact words: "I'm taking in a war guest. A little girl from London. Seven years old. She arrives tomorrow."

"I didn't know you'd volunteered," Mother said.

"I preferred not to tell anyone in advance, in case I was rejected. A maiden lady of my years might be viewed as unsuitable."

She turned to look at Peggy, and when Peggy felt Miss Putnam's stern eyes upon her, she shrank back against the sofa cushions.

"I hope you'll come to play with her," Miss Putnam said.

"Peggy would love to," said Mother, before Peggy had a chance to answer.

Miss Putnam's eyes flickered; she looked annoyed at Mother for speaking out of turn.

"What do you say, Peggy? You're old enough to speak for yourself."

"Oh, yes. I'd like to play with her."

Miss Putnam peered closely at Peggy, as if to make sure that she wasn't just saying what Mother wanted to hear. But when Peggy nodded her head and twisted her mouth into the grimace that passed for a smile since she had lost her two front teeth, Miss Putnam knew she meant it.

"I hoped you would," she said. "I'd like you to come for tea the day after tomorrow, at three o'clock, to meet Venetia."

"Her name is Venetia?" Peggy had never heard that name before.

"Venetia Lamb."

"Lamb! The same as me!"

"Yes. Quite a coincidence, isn't it?"

Peggy nodded her agreement, although she did not yet know what "coincidence" meant. She and Venetia had the same last name, and they were both seven years old. Maybe coincidence meant that they were like twins.

Although Peggy and Venetia shared a surname and a year of birth, they had little else in common. Venetia had golden ringlets, while Peggy's hair was dark brown and braided into pigtails fastened with rubber bands. Venetia's eyes were blue as the sky, but Peggy's were a mixed-up muddy green. Venetia's teeth were as even as two rows of pearls, while Peggy had a hole where one upper front tooth had been, and beside the hole a big tooth that was growing in crooked.

The scrapbook has a snapshot of Venetia and Peggy standing side by side. Peggy smiles when she looks at it. "Venetia was a fairy," she reflects, "and I was a gnome."

The scrapbook contains no memento of the afternoon tea when Peggy met Venetia. She remembers being puzzled because Venetia called sweaters *jumpers*, and cookies *biscuits*. In fact, every word that came out of her mouth sounded odd.

"You talk funny," said Peggy.

"I come from London," said Venetia. "Everybody there speaks as I do."

"I don't come from anywhere," Peggy confessed, feeling slightly ashamed. "I've lived here ever since my mother and father brought me home from the hospital."

"Hospital?" Venetia's blue eyes widened. "Were you hurt?"

"No. I was just getting born."

"In the hospital? Really?" Venetia seemed puzzled. "I was born at home—at least I think I was. My baby sister was born at home. So likely I was too."

"In Canada, people must go to the hospital to get a baby." Now Peggy felt important, for she knew something that Venetia didn't know. "The doctors store the babies there until a lady asks to have one. Then the doctors give it to her and she takes it home."

"Where do the doctors get the babies?" Venetia asked.

Peggy picked up another cookie and chewed vigorously. "I'm not sure," she admitted.

After finishing their afternoon tea—cookies and milk, not tea at all—they went to Venetia's bedroom to play with her toys.

Sitting on Venetia's pillow was a mangy stuffed bear. "That's Thomas," said Venetia. "I love him most because he was the only toy I could bring with me from England. Miss Putnam bought everything else." She waved towards a set of shelves that held crayons, construction paper, colouring books, a box of dominoes, a doll in a pink dress, ribbed slabs of Plasticine in many colours, and a new book of paper dolls. Peggy inspected the array as if she were visiting a toyshop.

"Lucky you," she said.

"What would you like to play with?"

"Can we play with the paper dolls?"

Venetia picked up the paper doll book and handed it to Peggy. The dolls were the Dionne Quintuplets, five identical cardboard girls in slightly different poses, all dressed in underwear. The dolls themselves were printed on the front and back covers of the book, their figures outlined with perforations for easy punching out. Their clothes were printed on the paper pages inside. The Quints had dresses for play, parties and church. Each dress had two shoulder tabs and two side tabs which, when folded over, would keep the dress from falling off.

Peggy and Venetia carefully punched out the dolls. Peggy decided that Yvonne was the prettiest. Venetia preferred Cecile, though both agreed that there was little reason for choosing one Quint over the other four.

"I saw the Quints last summer," Peggy said as they cut out the dresses. "We went to North Bay on our vacation. We had to line up for hours. Then we went along a hall that had special windows so we could watch the Quints but they couldn't see us."

"What were they doing?"

"Playing. They had their own playground, with swings and slides. They were dressed all the same, in blue skirts and white blouses. Two nurses took care of them. The nurses wore white uniforms. I wanted to play with the Quints, but it wasn't allowed. Mother said the Quints just speak French, anyway."

"Did they really look exactly alike?"

"Yes, exactly. When I got back to our trailer, I looked in the mirror and wondered what it would be like to have four sisters just the same as me."

"If I had four sisters," Venetia said softly, "I should never be lonely. The Quints are lucky."

"Mother says they're lucky just to be alive. When they were born, they were so tiny that it would take all five of them together to make a regular size baby like I was when I got born."

"I wonder why their mum and dad had so many at the same time."

"I don't know," said Peggy. "When our cat Spooky has kittens, she usually has five. But it's not the same as ladies having babies, because cats grow their kittens inside their tummies."

"Did you ever see kittens getting born?"

"Mother won't let me watch." Peggy leaned forward and lowered her voice. "Spooky hides in different places to have her kittens. Next time I'm going to find out where she goes so I can watch."

"Will you let me watch too?"

"Of course. I'll come and get you when it happens."

The paper Quints had many dresses—all matching—but no white blouses and blue skirts like the ones Peggy had seen them wearing. Peggy said that she and Venetia should make some.

Venetia got crayons and white paper from the shelf. "I expect that white blouses and blue skirts are their school uniform. At my school in England we wore grey skirts and blue jackets."

"We don't have uniforms at my school," said Peggy.

"Why not?"

"We just don't."

"What school do you go to?" Venetia asked.

"Earl Kitchener."

"That's too bad. I wish I could go to school with you, but I can't go there. Miss Putnam is sending me to Lady Byng because it's like the school I went to in England. She says my parents would be upset if I went to a state school."

"You'll have to wear an ugly purple uniform."

"Purple is my favourite colour," said Venetia. "I expect that I'll like Lady Byng. I wouldn't want to go to school with boys."

"It's not so bad," said Peggy. "The boys have their own entrance and their own washroom and they sit on the boys' side of the classroom. You don't have to talk to them if you don't want to."

"Do you talk to them?"

"Sometimes."

Venetia lowered her voice. "Did you ever see that thing boys have between their legs?"

"Yes," Peggy said. "I've seen my little brothers in the bath."

"I wonder," said Venetia, "why boys have that thing."

"It's so they can pee standing up."

"Why would anyone want to do that?"

Peggy shrugged. "Boys do. Some boys on our block have peeing contests in the back alley to see who can squirt the farthest."

"Really and truly?" said Venetia.

"I've seen them," said Peggy, "from my bedroom window." She felt her prestige rising. Venetia couldn't top that!

The cat was ready to give birth. Her flanks bulged. She walked around in circles, pushing her nose into tiny spaces.

"She's looking for a place to have the kittens," said Mother.

"I wonder where she'll have them this time?" said Peggy.

Spooky's last batch had been born in the linen cupboard, and the batch before that in Mother's lingerie drawer.

"I'll tell you where! In the basement. I've fixed up a cardboard carton with newspapers on the bottom, and that's where Spooky is going right now." Mother scooped up the cat in her arms and carried her away.

Peggy ran around the corner to Miss Putnam's house to tell Venetia. She rang the doorbell, but no one answered. She went into the garden. No one was there. Not wanting to waste any more time, Peggy hurried home. Mother was not in the kitchen to stop her from going to the basement. She opened the door and crept down the stairs.

Spooky was in the cardboard carton, and she was not alone. On the newspaper lay a black kitten, a white kitten, and a brindled grey. Peggy gazed in awe at their tiny pink feet tipped with minuscule claws and at their blunt little heads with sealed eyes.

Spooky's purr was as loud as a motor. She was sitting upright with her back to Peggy, busy with something between her hind legs. Then she moved sideways, allowing Peggy to see the grey, membranous sack that lay in front of her and watch as she ripped it open with her teeth. The sack contained an orange kitten. Spooky raised her head and stared at Peggy with her round yellow eyes. Then she lowered her head and began to lick the orange kitten.

Peggy reached out to touch it, and then changed her mind. "I'll come back later," she said to Spooky. All the way up the basement stairs, she could hear the cat's deep, vibrating purr.

Later in the day, Peggy called on Venetia. Peggy pretended not to notice that Venetia was wearing a purple tunic when she opened the door.

"Spooky's had her kittens. I came to get you, but you weren't home."

"I had to go to Lady Byng with Miss Putnam to pick up my uniform." Venetia looked at her sheepishly, almost with embarrassment. "I just tried it on to see how it looks."

"I hate purple," said Peggy. "I don't want you to go to

Lady Byng. I hate girls who go there. They're all stuck up."

"Miss Putnam says I'll make lots of friends."

"Then I suppose you won't play with me any more?"

"Of course I shall." Venetia hugged her. "You'll always be my best friend. I don't care what school you go to."

Peggy felt better. Overlooking the purple tunic, she accepted the offer of tea—which meant milk and cookies, as she now knew. Peggy and Venetia were silent as they ate. After they had finished, they went to Venetia's room.

"Want to play paper dolls?" Venetia asked.

"Okay."

Venetia took a big manila envelope from a shelf. She sat down on the floor and, opening the envelope slid out the Quints and their dresses. Peggy squatted beside her.

"Let's dress Cecile and Yvonne in their church clothes," Venetia said. "Let's pretend that the others got killed. Then Cecile and Yvonne can go to their funeral."

"How did they get killed?"

"In the bombing, of course."

"There isn't any bombing in Canada. Besides, none of the Quints are dead."

Venetia ignored her. She slipped Emily, Marie and Annette back into the envelope, which she then set on the floor in front of her.

"The envelope will be the graveyard. We'll use dominoes for tombstones. There have to be lots of tombstones because there are so many dead people. My best friend before you is in the graveyard. So are my Nana and Granddad. They all lived on the same street so their houses got hit at the same time. I went to my friend's funeral on Wednesday and to my grandparents' on Thursday. I cried and cried."

Peggy did not know what to say. She had never been to a funeral. Nobody she knew had ever died. She watched silently while Venetia fetched her box of dominoes from the toy shelves.

"Just imagine that there's a dead person under every domino," Venetia said while setting up the dominoes in neat rows. "Of course it's only their bodies; their souls have gone to heaven."

Peggy shivered. "I don't want to play funerals."

"Don't you? Well, what do you want to do?"

"I want to show you the kittens. That's why I called on you."

Venetia looked up. "Yes. That's a good idea. Kittens are much jollier than funerals."

While Venetia took off her purple tunic and put on her play clothes, Peggy picked up the dominoes and paper dolls.

"I'm glad that I found a new best friend," Venetia took Peggy's hand as they walked down the porch steps. "I was so very lonely after my last one died."

Peggy turned on the basement light and led Venetia down the steps. They tiptoed to the box. Spooky lay on her side with five tiny kittens whose noses were buried in the fur of her belly. One was black, one white, one brindled grey, one grey and white, and one orange.

"Quints!" said Venetia, "although they don't look alike." Spooky lifted her head and stared at the girls while they stroked her kittens. "What are you going to name them?"

"I don't know."

"You could name them after the Quints."

"What if some are boys?" Peggy asked.

"I don't imagine they'll know the difference."

There is a snapshot of Venetia and Peggy playing with the cat quints. Probably they all got new names after they were adopted, but Peggy remembers them as Marie, Cecile, Emily, Annette and Yvonne.

School began in September. Peggy walked to Earl Kitchener, but Venetia rode to Lady Byng in a bus that picked her up each morning and brought her home each afternoon. Peggy usually called on Venetia after school, and Venetia was just as nice as ever, despite the purple tunic.

"Do you like your school?" Peggy asked after a couple of weeks.

"Oh, yes! We play lots of games."

"Do you have many new friends?" Peggy asked awkwardly.

"The girls are nice. But none of them are best friends, the way you are."

Peggy got her first look at the nice girls a few days later when she called at Miss Putnam's house on her way home from school. As soon as the door opened, Peggy saw that the front hall was full of purple tunics. Above every tunic was a face, and every face turned toward Peggy.

One of the faces belonged to Venetia, who appeared embarrassed to see Peggy at the door. The expressions on the other faces ran the gamut from surprise to disbelief. All of them stared at Peggy's red corduroy dress. Then one little girl—a stocky redhead with freckles—said in a brave voice, "I'm not allowed to play with children from the public school."

There was silence. Venetia looked with anxious eyes from Peggy to the Lady Byng girls and back to Peggy again. Peggy still remembers the silence. She felt her own lack of purple with sudden shame, as if she had been caught naked, and her hands moved instinctively to hide as much of her red dress as she could, one arm across her chest and the other over her stomach.

"I guess I'd better go home," Peggy said.

The girls in purple tunics let out a sigh of relief. Peggy felt their eyes follow her down the porch steps. The door closed.

After that, Peggy started buying treats for Venetia. Venetia never asked her to, but it felt right. No matter how much she hated the purple tunic, Peggy knew that it made Venetia a superior person who was somehow more deserving. Whenever Peggy had a couple of pennies, she stopped at the grocery store on her way home from school to buy gumballs or licorice babies, one for herself and one for Venetia, who accepted these tributes gracefully. "You're my best friend," said Venetia, her mouth stuffed with candy. "You always will be."

Peggy was down in the basement playing with Spooky's kittens when she overheard Mother and Father talking in the kitchen. Mother said, "If Peggy went to Lady Byng, she wouldn't have these problems."

Peggy crawled under the staircase so that she could listen without being seen.

"What problems?" Father asked.

"Miss Putnam says that Venetia's other friends don't accept her."

"That's their problem, not Peggy's."

"You're missing the point. If she went to Lady Byng, they would accept her."

"Does Peggy say she wants to go there?" said Father.

"Not in so many words. But she's obviously jealous because Venetia goes to Lady Byng, and she doesn't."

Peggy, scrunched under the stairs, felt like screaming. She did not want to go to Lady Byng. She was not jealous. Except for Venetia, she hated the girls in purple tunics.

"Well," said Father, "you know how she feels better than I do. Maybe in a couple of years we'll be able to afford it."

"You've always been prejudiced against private schools," said Mother.

"I don't deny it. I dislike the idea of extra privilege. As for standards, Earl Kitchener is a good school."

"Miss Putnam is worried about Peggy. She's afraid that the riff-raff at Earl Kitchener will be a bad influence."

"Miss Putnam should keep her views to herself."

Peggy turns another page in the scrapbook. Here is the invitation to Venetia's birthday party. A big, red number "8" with a bunch of balloons. In Miss Putnam's careful handwriting: "Venetia Lamb invites you to her party. November 2, 3 to 5 p.m."

Why on earth did Mother have to keep that?

"I don't want to go," Peggy said.

"Don't be silly," said Mother. "Venetia will be hurt if you don't."

"All the other girls will be from Lady Byng. They don't want to play with me and I don't want to play with them."

"Nonsense. You're going anyway. We don't want to offend Miss Putnam."

"She won't care. She only asked me to play with Venetia because there wasn't anybody else around."

"That's not true. Miss Putnam is very fond of you."

Mother took Peggy to Eaton's to buy a party dress. The one Mother liked was pink organdy, with ruffles and little velvet bows. It was probably the most expensive in the store.

"She'll try on this one," Mother said to the saleslady.

When Peggy looked at herself in the mirror, she felt silly, as if she were wearing a Hallowe'en costume. This was a gown for a princess, not a skinny girl with pigtails and scabby knees.

"Exquisite," the saleslady said.

"You'll be the best-dressed girl at the party," Mother said with a determined glint in her eyes.

To go with the dress, Mother bought pink hair ribbons, pink knee socks, and shiny white Mary Janes. The night before the party, she tied up Peggy's hair in rags to force it to curl.

The birthday gift was the only thing that Peggy had been allowed to choose. Mother thought that a music box would be nicer, but Peggy insisted on buying a Shirley Temple paper doll. She thought it was perfect because Shirley Temple's ringlets were like Venetia's, although not such a pretty colour. The doll was printed on cardboard with a flocked surface to help the dresses stay in place. And there were sheets of paper dresses to cut out.

Mother wrapped the gift in white tissue paper, with a pink ribbon tied into a bow, and a sprig of silk lily-of-the-valley flowers that she had tucked away in her sewing box.

"Can't I just take Venetia's present to her afterwards?" Peggy pleaded.

"No," said Mother. "You're going to the party. You'll have fun once you get there."

Peggy trudged around the corner to Miss Putnam's house. She was standing outside the front door gathering courage, when another girl came thumping up the steps behind her. The girl glanced at Peggy, "Oh, hello," she said.

"Hello," said Peggy.

The girl rang the doorbell. The door opened, and the girl walked in. Peggy followed, clutching her gift. The other girl swept into the living room and in an instant merged into the squealing throng gathered around Venetia.

Peggy watched from a corner of the front hall. The living room was strung with streamers of pink and white crêpe paper. Hanging from the centre light fixture was a cluster of pink balloons. Little girls wearing muslin frocks twirled and jumped and ran around hugging each other. Peggy recognized the freckled redhead who was not allowed to play with children from the public school.

No one else was dressed in organdy with ruffles and velvet bows.

For a long time—at least it seemed like a long time— Peggy watched from her corner. Her eyes felt hot, and she could hardly breathe because of the big, sore lump in her throat. She had to escape before she started to cry. She had to get out of there, back to her house. Hide in her room. Crawl into bed and pull the covers over her head. Anything but stay at this party, where nobody wanted her and where she did not want to be.

Peggy took a tiny step, then another. Step by step, she sidled toward the front door, her eyes fixed upon Venetia. If her friend would only look at her, wave to her, smile and call her name, then Peggy would rush to her side and claim the right to be at this party. But Venetia had not noticed her cowering in the hall.

Peggy turned the doorknob and slipped out the door. Taking a deep breath, she walked down the porch steps, out to the sidewalk, and up the street. Just before the corner of Orchard Hill, she stopped at the sewer grating by the curb. She peered down between the metal bars at the dark sewer water, then leaned over and carefully dropped Venetia's birthday gift through the grate. It slipped between the bars like a slice of bread going into a toaster and hit the water with a splat. Peggy did not wait to see whether Shirley Temple floated or sank.

Of course she got in trouble at home. Mother wanted to march her right back to the party. But when Peggy said that the birthday gift was down the sewer, Mother gave up that idea and sent Peggy to her room.

Venetia called on Peggy the next day. She stood on Peggy's porch, wearing her play clothes.

"Why didn't you come to my party?"

"I got sick."

"That's too bad. I missed you."

"You got lots of other friends."

Venetia scuffed her feet on the doormat. "Don't you want to be my best friend any more?"

This was the moment when she should have invited Venetia to come in. There was a new batch of kittens to admire, for Spooky consistently gave birth to three litters every year. But Peggy felt mean. She wanted Venetia to know what it was like to be shut outside.

"I guess so," Peggy said. "But I can't play now. I have to clean up my room."

Peggy never played with Venetia again. Venetia called on her several more times, but Peggy always made excuses. For the rest of the school year, she took a different route to and from school in order to avoid walking by Miss Putnam's house.

That summer, Peggy's parents bought a house in a different part of town, in a nice neighbourhood where everybody was the same. All of the children went to the same public school, and none had cooties in their hair.

The light outside is failing. Peggy switches on the table lamp beside her chair. She flips through the second scrapbook bearing her name, the one that records her progress right up to her wedding day. There are no mementoes of Venetia in this book.

After Peggy's family had moved away from Orchard Hill, ten years passed before she encountered another Lady Byng girl. This one was an Old Girl, which meant that she had graduated from Lady Byng with her Junior Matriculation—the highest level of studies offered there. The Old Girl (who was eighteen years of age) was attending the public high school for her Senior Matriculation.

"Do you remember an English girl named Venetia Lamb?" Peggy asked her one day. "She must have been in your year at Lady Byng."

"Venetia Lamb? I think so. Blond? Blue eyes?"

"Yes. That's her."

"She went back to England after the war. I think she lives in London, but she hasn't kept in touch with anyone. She didn't make close friends at Lady Byng."

Peggy closes the scrapbook and sets it down with the others. Tomorrow she will decide what to do with them. Most likely she'll repack them in the carton and shove it under her bed.

She wonders, What does Venetia look like now? A vision of golden ringlets crosses her mind. She tries to picture Venetia at sixty-five, but cannot do it. Does she ever think of me? And if she does, am I forgiven?

The Quilt

When Judy came over today, she brought me a new mohair throw. "There," she said, "this will keep you a lot warmer than that old quilt you've been using." She tucked it around my legs. I stroked the soft, silky wool. Light as a feather and very pretty—deep rose and dark green. I like those colours.

Knowing Judy, there had to be something behind it. Everything she does for me is for my own good, of course, and I'm lucky to have a daughter who cares. But all the time I wonder what she's up to.

She thinks I don't notice, but—merciful heavens—does she imagine that my mind is as weak as my legs? Judy is forever giving me advice on how to handle my own affairs. Selling my house was her idea. I don't deny that it made sense.

"Mom," she said, "you're eighty years old and you live alone. You don't need four bedrooms, three bathrooms and half an acre of lawn that has to be mowed every week."

"Maybe you're right," I said. "It doesn't make much sense, does it?"

Yet I did love the house. It had meant so much to Bill. That's why I held on to it for twenty years after he died. The house was his pride and joy. It showed the world how far he'd come. When he was a boy, nobody around Hay Bay had indoor plumbing. Backhouse behind the kitchen garden. Chamber pot under the bed. When Bill gave visitors a house tour, those three bathrooms were the star attraction.

"Of course I'm right." Judy put on that tight, self-satisfied smile. "Keeping the house must cost you a fortune. Taxes. Insurance. Heating. And what do you pay the man who cuts the grass?"

That was Judy. Prying, prying. Digging into my finances. Why did she need to know how I spent every penny? Did she think I wasn't competent? Or was she worried about me spending her inheritance?

But she was right about selling the house. The timing was good, too. Five years later, I wouldn't have got two hundred and fifty thousand. That's two hundred and fifty thousand net, after commission and legal fees. A lot more than it would fetch in today's market. I was glad to get the house off my hands. All I need is a one-bedroom apartment. And my quilt.

Where did Judy put my quilt? There aren't a lot of places where it could vanish.

"That quilt is my book of memories," I'd told Judy many a time. Better than old photograph albums. Snapshots are only grey and white images—at least the snapshots I care about are grey and white—showing one single moment. Well, I guess that's the idea, isn't it? Snap! You shoot the moment. Capture it, dead or alive, on a shiny rectangle of paper.

Ah, but a quilt! Every patch of fabric tells a story. Take the grey flannel squares. Bill's good suit. He bought that when they elected him reeve. Bill needed something nice to wear to township council meetings. He wore it for a long time, until it got too tight. The Jessop men always got heavy. First they got fat, then they got bald, and then they got a heart attack. Why had I thought that Bill would be an exception? He was sixty-two when he died. That was more than twenty years ago.

I still miss that dear, sweet man! I touch those grey flannel squares and feel Bill in his suit. Big shoulders. Strong arms to hold me. Well, I'm not going to dwell on it.

Then there are the navy blue squares. Tim's blazer. Wasn't he the handsome fellow in that! We bought him the blazer for his high school graduation. It cost a bundle, but Tim said he would be able wear it to dances at university, and to weddings. Brand new when I cut it up for squares. He wore it once.

Oh, where is my quilt?

Judy keeps reading those articles about coping with elderly parents: "Choosing a Retirement Home," "Best Buys in Planned Funerals," "When to Get Power of Attorney," and "Is Revenue Canada Your Heir?"

I read them too, but I don't tell her. I have to keep ahead of Judy somehow. Sit down with your old father/mother, they say. Be tactful but frank.

Judy tried it. "Mom, maybe it's time for you to tell me about your assets."

"What assets?" I pretended not to understand. "Do you mean my big brown eyes?"

"No!"

"My intelligence, then?"

"Oh, stop it," she said. "You know perfectly well what I mean. Bank accounts. Investments. Where's your safety deposit box? I should know where things are in case something happens to you."

"What exactly do you have in mind?" I asked her. "Are you planning for something to happen?" Judy backed off. She could never bring herself to use the word "death." Not to me, anyhow. I felt sorry for her, she looked so embarrassed.

The navy blue squares break my heart. Bill said not to use them, but I wasn't going to throw away my last good memory of Tim. All the other kids had got out of the car before the train hit. Stalled on the tracks. Tim was sure he could get it started. That's what his friends said. He didn't want to wreck his dad's car. As if the damn car was worth Tim's life. Something was wrong with the carburetor. That car was always stalling. Bill should have traded it in long before.

I can touch the navy blue squares and see Tim up there on the stage receiving his scholarship. Curly black hair. Broad shoulders like his dad's. Best-looking boy in the graduating class. Bill and I sat in the front row of the auditorium. Judy may have been with us, but I'm not sure. Bill was bursting with pride to see his son shake hands with Mr. Fletcher, the Chairman of the School Board. "Congratulations," Mr. Fletcher said when he handed Tim the envelope. "You're a credit to Hay Bay."

As Tim turned to leave the stage, he looked at me and smiled.

Afterwards, we sat around the kitchen table and ate the cake that I had baked and decorated with "Congratulations Tim!" in chocolate icing. That's the last cake I ever decorated. Judy wanted me to do her wedding cake. Maybe I should have, but I couldn't work up enough enthusiasm.

Tim read the award letter to us. Four years free tuition at the University of Toronto, plus five thousand dollars cash. That's pretty good for a farm boy whose parents left school at sixteen. It's a shame Tim never got to use his scholarship. He wanted to be a doctor.

I can touch the navy blue squares and remember Tim the way he was at eighteen. At least, I could touch them if I had the quilt here on my lap. It's not in the linen cupboard. It's not on my bed. I certainly hope that Judy hasn't put it in the wash. She has good intentions, but sometimes I wish that she would leave well enough alone.

It was thirty years ago that I made the quilt. We were still on the farm—that was before we sold out to the developer and bought the house in Napanee. I had the squares all pieced together and ready to quilt, when I said to Bill, "I'm going to have an old-fashioned quilting bee, like my mother used to. There are women around here who haven't been to a quilting bee since they were girls."

"Good idea," Bill said. He was still reeve then, before his second heart attack. Bit of a glad-hander, Bill was, always thinking about the next election. "Be sure to let the newspaper know about it so they can send a photographer."

Sure enough, the *Napanee Beaver* showed up to take a picture of us ladies. I still have that picture in a shoebox somewhere. The newsprint was yellow and falling apart last time I looked at it.

Bill fetched my quilting frame from the attic. He'd made it for me when we were first married, and was very proud of it.

"We'll set it up in the kitchen," I said.

So we pushed the table aside to make room for the frame, and then put out chairs all along the sides. Before the women arrived, Bill and I had attached the pieced-together squares to the frame, with the cotton batting to line it, and then the backing. The backing was dark red, a lovely warm colour.

There were eight women, some of them neighbours and others from the church that Bill and I attended. Not one was under forty years old. Even thirty years ago, young women didn't do quilting. Everything store-bought. Judy couldn't do a decent quilting stitch to save her life.

We chatted the whole time—talked about recipes and who'd had a baby and who'd died. Stitch, stitch, stitch all day long. When we had finished quilting, we tidied everything up and served the sandwiches and pies that the women had brought with them. I put the big kettle on the stove to make tea for everybody.

I was happy that day. My fingers were sore, but I was truly happy.

A few weeks later Judy saw the quilt when she came home for the weekend. Judy worked in an office in Kingston. She was about twenty at the time, finished school. Never went to college. In this family, Tim had all the brains as well as the good looks.

When she looked at the quilt her eyes narrowed. "Why aren't there any squares for me?" There was that chip on her shoulder, as usual.

"Oh, there must be," I said.

"Not one."

When I took a good look, I saw that she was right. "Well," I said, "I guess there weren't any old clothes of yours in the scrap bag. No need to take on about it."

It was like Judy to make something out of nothing. She never did appreciate that quilt.

We sold the farm the year after that. The developer paid a good price. One hundred thousand dollars looked like a fortune in 1972. Bill thought he'd struck gold. But I realize now that if we'd waited a few years, we could have got a million for two hundred acres with half-a-mile of Lake Ontario shoreline. After selling the farm, we moved to Napanee and bought the big house. Bill died two years later.

Judy wanted me to buy a condominium after I sold the

house in Napanee.

"No," I said. "I don't want to own any more property. I'm going to rent an apartment until I'm ready to check into a retirement home. And I don't need any help in finding what I want."

Judy spluttered a bit. She always wants to put her oar in. "There's not much to choose from in Napanee."

"Who says it has to be Napanee? I'm moving to the big city."

She turned pale. "Toronto?"

"No. Kingston."

She looked relieved. "That's good," she said. "It will be easy for me to drop in a couple of times a week to check on you. I can take you shopping and to doctor's appointments."

I felt like saying I was still capable of driving myself, but that would have started a row. Judy needs to feel useful. Fifty years old. Married. No kids. Not enough to occupy her time.

You should have seen her face when she saw the apartment. Uniformed doorman. Oil paintings in the lobby. Every luxury known to man. "Mom, you can't afford this!" she said.

"Oh, can't I?"

I had never told her what I got for the house, but I'm pretty sure she found out somehow.

"Put the money from selling the house into Guaranteed Investment Certificates," had been her advice. "Then your capital will be safe, and you can live comfortably on the interest."

Well, I didn't want to live comfortably. For the first time in my life, I wanted to live in style.

If Judy knew that I'd put two hundred thousand into a Guaranteed Single Life Annuity! Well, I don't know what she'd say. For the rest of my life, $2,168 goes automatically into my bank account every month. That's double what I would have got from those GIC's she wanted me to buy. Of course, the money dies with me. At my death the insurance company keeps the capital. Nothing left for Judy.

It isn't as if she'll ever really be in need. Judy has a husband to support her. And she'll still get the fifty thousand I've sewn into the quilt. All in one thousand dollar bills. They were crisp and new when I got them from the bank. I wore them inside my brassiere for a week to soften them up. Twenty-five on each side. I have a fifty thousand dollar bosom, I said to myself. Why, I bet even Mae West can't beat that!

I sewed the money into the quilt five years ago when Judy was complaining about the backing looking all shabby and worn. "Buy me the fabric," I said, "and I'll put on a new backing." So she did. Dark blue. It looked really nice. The same shade as the quilt squares from my old plaid skirt. That was a lovely skirt. I used to wear it when I went for walks with Bill … when I could walk. A long time ago.

You know, I hate to say this, but I'm afraid that I've seen the last of my quilt. I think that Judy tossed it out when she gave me this store-bought throw. A few days ago, she was making nasty comments about my quilt. Said it was only fit for the garbage. Oh, yes. She would do that. Judy doesn't like old things.

After the Game

Galina woke up to find herself on a bare mattress in a bare room. The ceiling sloped, and overhead was a brown stain shaped like the map of Australia. The air reeked of stale beer, sweat and musk. The single window was closed. Red maple leaves fluttered on the other side of the dirty glass.

She raised herself on one elbow and winced. Even this slight movement of her body was painful. Her belly hurt. Her thighs hurt. Her crotch hurt. And she was cold. Except for her socks, she was naked from the waist down.

When she turned her head, she saw that her jeans were tidily folded on the floor, with her panties on top and her shoes placed neatly side by side.

Galina remembered the football game, and afterwards the crowd at Grubby's, and everyone goofing around. Oh,

God! How much had she drunk? Who had she been with? And what was in those drinks?

She got to her feet. Sticky warm liquid tinged with blood ran down the inside of her thighs. Galina got a tissue from a pocket of her jeans to wipe it from her skin. She pressed the tissue against her crotch to blot the rest, and then sat on the mattress to put on her panties, jeans and shoes.

Through the open door Galina could see across the hall into another room. In it were a dresser, a desk, a bookcase, and an unmade bed. On the floor lay a jumble of jockey shorts, sweatpants, sweatshirts and tube socks.

She looked at her watch. Ten o'clock. She checked the pockets of her jeans. Wallet, lipstick, comb. Nothing missing. She listened for sounds that would signal another person's presence in the house. She heard the hum of a refrigerator motor somewhere below.

The floorboards squeaked as she left the room, and the stairs creaked as she tiptoed down. On the next floor were four doors, two closed and two that stood open to reveal bedrooms similar to those on the top storey. Galina held her breath as she edged her way down a short flight of steps to the landing. She stopped, looked around, then descended the rest of the way.

At the bottom of the staircase, empty pizza boxes, sport shoes, beer bottles, and pieces of a shattered plate littered the hall. The living room showed evidence of an egg fight— whites and broken yolks dribbling down the walls, crushed shells lying at the base. A drunken student passed out on the sofa would have completed the scene. But no one was there.

The refrigerator hummed noisily as Galina opened the front door.

When she got out to the sidewalk, she looked around. She was on Earl Street, the heart of the university ghetto, in front of a house that she had never entered before. A broken-down sofa stood on the porch, bicycles were chained to the railings, beer bottles lay on the lawn. She had no idea who lived there.

Galina walked directly back to her dormitory. There were few people on the streets, only a scattering of neatly dressed couples on their way to church. It must be Sunday. The game had been played Saturday afternoon. So she had been in the house overnight.

She knew that she should go to the University Health Service, if it was open on Sunday, or to Emergency at the hospital. But then people would question her, touch her, smell her. She shuddered. No. Unbearable. First she had to wash.

As soon as she got to her room, she stripped, put on her robe, and went down the hall to the showers. She turned on the water as hot as she could bear. Standing in the hiss and steam, she soaped and rinsed her body. Then she turned the temperature control dial the opposite way and let the icy jet lash her skin until it numbed. When Galina stepped out, shivering, she felt almost clean.

She got dressed, then took the clothes that she had been wearing down to the laundry room, put them into a washer, and set it for "extra-soiled." Galina returned to her room. The only food she had was a Coffee Crisp chocolate bar. She made do with that. She had to eat. Her mind was numb, but her body made its usual demands.

Galina crawled under the green plaid futon that covered her bed and curled up in a loose fetal position. Now she must try to think. She'd had sex, remembered or not. It was rape, or she would not feel so sore. She pressed her hands against her stomach. A spasm of shame and rage ran through her. This body was hers. The violator must not go unpunished.

Her eyes went to the telephone on her desk. Should she call the police? Forget it! There was no point. How could she report it? Maybe she hadn't been raped. How could she prove what had happened—what she thought had happened? All she remembered was going to Grubby's with Mavis and Paula after the football game. Then things went fuzzy. If she wanted to find out more, she'd have to ask her friends. Did she want to do that? No.

Someone knocked at her door, a polite gentle rapping. Galina did not answer. It happened again, and again she ignored the noise until whoever it was gave up and went away. Then Mavis and Paula came to the door. Galina recognized their voices. When she didn't answer, they shouted and kicked the door.

"Are you all right?" Mavis called.

"Open up! We know you're in there," Paula yelled. They stopped the racket. Galina heard them talking about overdoses and comas. When Mavis said they'd better fetch a caretaker with the key, Galina forced herself to get up and open the door.

"I was having a nap."

"I guess you were," said Paula. "After last night."

They came into the room without being invited, as they always did. Mavis flopped onto the bed, and Paula onto the one easy chair. Galina turned to face them, her hand still on the doorknob.

"Yeah. I was out late."

"Late!" said Mavis. "This morning when we called for you to go to breakfast, you weren't here."

"I must have been too sound asleep to hear you."

"The door was locked," said Paula. "You lock your door when you go out, not when you go to bed."

Galina made herself laugh. "Okay. I confess. I wasn't here. I went to a party and ended up crashing on somebody's couch."

"What was his name?" Paula asked.

"Who?" Galina tightened her grip on the doorknob.

"The somebody with the couch." Paula grinned. "Tall, dark and handsome? The guy you left Grubby's with? The way he was wrapped all over you, I bet you didn't need a blanket on that couch."

Galina felt her stomach twist. She grabbed at the first male name she could think of. "Brian," she said. "Brian Somebody-with-a-Couch." She forced another laugh, easier this time.

"You were high," said Paula. "What else besides his last name do you forget?"

"If I knew what I forgot, then it wouldn't be forgotten, would it?" Galina heard panic in her laughter. Did they? It was hard to act normal when all she wanted was to get them out of her room. A worried expression replaced the smile on Mavis' face.

"We just wondered if you wanted to go to the movies," she said, getting up from the bed. "When you wouldn't answer the door, we got scared."

"Thanks," Galina said, herding them out and closing the door behind them. Tall, dark and handsome. Who was he? She sat down at her desk and buried her face in her hands. Why couldn't she remember?

In the morning she left by the rear door and walked a round-about route to the lecture hall. She took a seat in the middle of the back row, opened a textbook, and pretended to concentrate so that no one would talk to her.

After the lecture, she returned to the residence by the same roundabout route and went straight up to her room. Mavis dropped in. Brisk, efficient Mavis was a Nursing Science student, always interested in the health of her friends. "You look lousy," she said.

"I'm just tired," said Galina. She let Mavis take her blood pressure. Mavis said it was something over something and looked satisfied. Before leaving, she asked, "Is Brian going to call you?"

"Ah, Brian. No, I don't think so. We had a good time, but, well ... he's not my type."

Galina began to use the cafeteria at off hours to avoid other people. When the weekend rolled around, she locked her door and pretended to be out. On Saturday Mavis and Paula wanted her to go to Grubby's again. Galina wasn't interested. "I've had some bad news from home," she said. This lie served her purpose. Paula and Mavis knew not to pry.

Galina never went back to Grubby's. She avoided Earl Street. Whenever a tall, dark-haired, good-looking guy glanced at her, she turned away.

One afternoon, when she had left her table in the library to go to the washroom, she came back to find a note tucked into her copy of *Paradise Lost*. "I'm sorry," was all it said. She looked around. About fifty people were in the library. Half of them were men, several dark and more or less good-looking. Unless they stood up, she couldn't tell which were tall. Was the note writer one of them? Or had he sneaked away?

When Galina's period was late, she persuaded herself that shock was the cause. She let another month go. By the time she had vomited on five successive mornings, she knew that it was time to grasp the nettle and visit the University Health Service.

After taking a seat in the crowded reception area, she had to wait half an hour. Other students waiting all appeared to have bad colds. They coughed, sneezed, and rubbed red noses with balled-up tissues.

Galina looked at her watch. Her next class started at one o'clock. She didn't want to miss it. She stood and was about to leave when a counsellor called her name.

The counsellor was frank and friendly. Professional.

"Have you told your boyfriend?"

Galina shook her head. "I don't have a boyfriend. No one special."

The counsellor didn't look shocked. "If you're going to be sexually active, you need to take precautions."

"It wasn't like that," said Galina. "It was … different."

The counsellor calmly outlined Galina's options. Abortion would be simplest. She obviously expected Galina to choose that, "unless you are a Catholic, of course, and then …"

"I'm not a Catholic. I don't have any religion."

The counsellor looked her in the eye. "Think it over, then. Make your decision as soon as you can."

Galina nodded.

The interview was at an end. It was too late to go to her one o'clock class. Better grab a bite to eat. She walked slowly, head lowered. The sidewalk was slippery with wet leaves clinging to the damp concrete. It had rained during the night, but now the air was clear.

She wished that she had someone to talk to. Well, she had Paula and Mavis. Why couldn't she talk to them? It wasn't that she didn't trust them—she did. But she could not speak about waking up on that mattress in that shabby room.

She would have an abortion, of course. What else? Otherwise, she could imagine the things people would say: "Galina Morris is having a baby, and nobody knows who the father is."

A baby. At this very moment, amazing things were happening inside her body. Minuscule cells were dividing, forming limbs, organs, eyes, a brain. Sex organs too. This beginning life was already male or female, boy or girl. Well, better not to think about that; she had already made her decision. It was time to get lunch and go to class. Then she would call Health Services to make an appointment for the abortion.

"Lady, can you get our ball?" A young boy's voice, loud and shrill.

Galina jumped. She had not noticed that she was outside a schoolyard. Six feet away, on the other side of a high, chain-link fence, stood a boy, perhaps twelve years old, pointing to a football in the gutter beside her.

"No problem." She picked it up, balanced it for a moment and hurled it over the fence, the ball sailing in a beautiful arc. The boy had to run back thirty feet to catch it.

Galina stood watching the children play. Little girls skipped rope on one side of the schoolyard; boys raced and threw footballs on the other. A bell clanged them in from recess. Galina waited until the last straggler had disappeared before she walked on.

In the cafeteria Galina picked up her usual lunch of hamburger, fries and a Coke. Then she put the Coke back and selected milk.

It was nearly two o'clock. She carried her tray between two rows of tables in the almost empty cafeteria, looking for a clean spot to set the tray down. Finally, she sat at a table where she could look out the window, though this table was as sticky as the rest. She ate half of the hamburger and picked at her fries. Everything tasted greasy.

Other students came in. She heard them talking to each other about their courses. She was sitting with her back to them. When she had finished her milk, she kept thinking that she would leave, but did not until after they had left. Then she carried her tray to the waste bin and dumped the rest of her lunch. She looked at her watch. There was time to get to her three o'clock lecture. But instead of going to class, she went back to her room and lay down.

Galina started going to the Law School Library to study. It was at the other end of campus, where she knew nobody. The law students ignored her; and she ignored them.

She liked it here—the long oak tables, the high ceilings and the tall bare windows that let in the afternoon light. Above the windows hung portraits of former Deans of Law—men with wise, understanding faces. Their compassionate eyes watched as she worked. She wished that she could talk to them, as her grandmother talked to her icons of holy saints. Galina would tell them about her misfortune, and they would counsel her on what to do.

Outside the library windows, the maple trees had lost their leaves. The naked branches waited, their buds locked in hard calyxes, for the coming of spring.

One Saturday evening a student in a yellow Faculty of Engineering jacket sat across from her. He had a high forehead and a frizz of blond hair that was already receding. He glanced over to see what she was reading. *Measure for Measure*.

"You're not a law student," he said. "Why do you come here?"

"Why do you? You're not a law student either."

"I can concentrate here. And it stays open late."

He did not disturb her while she studied. At eleven o'clock, when the librarian started to turn out the lights, they both gathered up their books.

"I'll walk you to your dorm," he said.

"I know my way."

"For your safety."

Galina couldn't be bothered arguing. "It's up to you." Probably he was harmless, but how could she be sure? The man who had taken her to the house on Earl Street must have looked harmless too. Galina put on her coat. She had keys in her pocket. She would clutch them in her fist, shafts between her fingers, if he touched her.

They walked side by side, keeping a space between them—about six inches—as if by consensus. When they neared Grubby's, she was afraid that he might invite her to go in for a beer. He didn't. He didn't even ask her name.

The following Saturday evening she encountered him again in the Law School Library, already working when she arrived at eight o'clock. When he looked up, she said, "What's an engineer doing here on a Saturday night?"

"You need someone to walk you home." His manner was polite. "My name is Steve Connor."

"I'm Galina Morris." She hadn't wanted to give her name and felt annoyed for having yielded to the habit of politeness.

"What kind of name is Galina?"

"Russian. My great-grandmother was a countess."

"Then you're an aristocrat."

"I think not. After she got to Canada, she married a pig farmer. But my parents had some hopes for me."

As they passed Grubby's, the door opened and a crowd of students spilled onto the sidewalk. Steve took Galina's arm and guided her across the street. This was the first time he had touched her. As soon as they reached the other side, he dropped his hand. When they got to the dormitory, he looked at her gravely and said, "I never go to Grubby's anymore."

"Oh? Don't you?"

Anymore? Steve Connor—blond and plain—was not the man. But did he know something of that shameful night?

Galina went straight to her room. No longer would she use the Law School Library. She did not intend to be anywhere that he could easily find her again.

But he did find her. Three days later, he was waiting outside the Arts Building when she emerged from class, and he crossed the campus at her side. "So you've given up the Law Library? I looked for you last Saturday."

"I work in my room now. It's safer."

Galina didn't dislike him. If things had been different, she would have chatted with him, maybe gone for coffee. The word "mechanical" was sewn onto the sleeve of his yellow jacket. It did not seem appropriate. Mechanical had a hard, inhuman sound. He seemed to be a warm person.

The next morning, as she left for the cafeteria, she saw him standing on the sidewalk. Galina went back inside and took a different door. So far, Steve had asked nothing of her, but something was coming. If she met him again, she would tell him to leave her alone.

She did not see him for the whole week of mid-term exams. November's first snow had fallen when, returning from class one dark afternoon, she found him waiting in front of the residence. "What are you doing here?"

"I want to talk to you."

"I'm going inside," she said. "It's freezing out here."

"Just a minute. There's something I need to say to you."

"No!"

He grabbed her arm, but as she pulled away, she was suddenly aware that he cared about her, and she felt sorry for him. "Come inside," she said. "We can talk in the common room." He followed her, walking a pace behind.

Although it was warm indoors, she kept her coat done up. She led him to a corner of the room where there were no chairs. "Well?" she asked.

A flush spread over his face. "What I want to say is that things happen to people that they don't plan. Sometimes you're in the wrong place at the wrong time. It can change everything. You know what I mean?"

"No. I don't. And I don't want to discuss it. But I have a question: do you remember telling me that you don't go to Grubby's anymore?"

"I remember."

"Anymore since when?"

"You know."

"Is that why you keep following me? If it is, then stop or I'll report you to the campus police. There are laws against stalking."

"This isn't stalking." He stared at the floor, refusing to meet her eyes.

"What else would you call it? Wherever I go, you keep showing up."

"Maybe I can help."

"The only way you can help is to leave me alone."

She turned to move away from him, but he shouted, "Wait!" From his jacket pocket he pulled out a file card and handed it to her. She glanced at it. He had written down a phone number.

"I don't need this." She tried to give it back to him, but his hands were in his pockets. Galina dropped the piece of paper on the floor and walked away.

At Christmas Galina went home. For three weeks she contemplated telling her mother what had happened, but never did.

As soon as she got back to campus, she wrote a letter home. In it she told her parents that she was pregnant and begged for their understanding. She said nothing about the circumstances, leaving them to imagine an unsuitable boy or a married man or some disastrous entanglement from which she had escaped, though at a painful cost.

If she'd had a stamp, she would have mailed the letter. At least she thought she would have mailed it. It sat on her desk for two weeks, and then she threw it away. Her parents would find out soon enough.

Galina did not buy maternity clothes. She went to bargain stores for loose-fitting dresses in the extra-large size. These drooped from her shoulders. The professors gave her second glances. Male students avoided her. So did most of the girls.

Mavis and Paula were disgusted. "Why do you dress like that?" said Mavis. "You could get some nice maternity clothes. I can't figure why you want to look like a bag lady."

"Are you trying to punish yourself?" asked Paula.

Galina hadn't thought of it that way. "Maybe," she said. "You study psychology. What do you think?"

"Galina, you're a textbook case—full of unresolved anger that you've turned against yourself. I don't know how you got in this mess. I suppose it was after the football game, when you left Grubby's with that Brian guy. Ever since then, you've been acting so weird!"

Galina shook her head. "His name wasn't Brian, at least as far as I know. I don't have a clue who he was."

"God!" said Mavis. "Rohypnol."

"What?" Galina must have looked puzzled.

"You know. A roofie. The date rape drug. Why didn't you go to the hospital?"

Galina looked away. Shrugged.

"Hell!" Paula snorted. "It wasn't your fault."

"Tests could have detected Rohypnol in your bloodstream for seventy-two hours," said Mavis. "There might have been witnesses. Maybe the police could have laid charges. At the very least, the hospital would have given you a morning-after pill."

"Even after you'd left it for a couple of months," said Paula, "you still could've had an abortion and put it all behind you."

"No, I couldn't," said Galina.

"So what happens now?"

"I'll have the baby."

"That's great," said Paula. "Now you hate yourself. A year from now, you'll hate the baby."

Alone in her room, Galina looked at herself in the mirror on the back of the door. She hated what she saw: a short, dumpy girl with mousy brown hair and a bulging belly. "I hope you'll take after me," she addressed the bulge. "But even if you don't, I won't hate you." The baby kicked, and Galina felt the moving bump that might have been a shoulder or a knee. "It isn't your fault."

She sat at her desk, opened a book but could not concentrate. Paula was right about her anger. She was filled with rage, boiling up steam like her mother's pressure cooker, and it had to escape. "Oh, shit!" she said, and slammed the book shut. She stood up, paced in quick circles around the room, then closed her fist and punched the wall. Drops of blood welled from her knuckles. What a stupid thing to do! But somebody had to be punished.

Steve caught up with her crossing the campus. It was spring, and warm. The first time in months that he had seen her not wearing a coat. "You're pregnant," he blurted out.

"Big surprise."

He stood on the path, blocking her way. "I didn't know."

"It's not your problem. I told you to leave me alone."

A deep flush spread over his face. "Maybe it is."

"Oh, let me by. I don't want to talk about it. I just want to forget the whole thing." She tried to shove past him, but he put out a hand to stop her.

"Well, you can't. Isn't that obvious? Who do you think you are, Tess of the D'Urbervilles?"

She laughed bitterly. "Do you think you're Angel Clare?"

"Me?" His face twisted into a grimace. "I'll tell you who I am. I'm the coward who hid in his bedroom while the others took you upstairs."

"Others?" Her knees turned to rubber.

"Don't you remember?"

"Others?"

"The five other guys in my house—where I live on Earl Street."

"Five? Five?"

"They were taking you upstairs and invited me to join them. I said, 'Count me out.'"

"The house was empty when I woke up."

"No, I was still there. The others cleared out so you wouldn't see them. They were scared."

"And you?"

"After they'd gone, I went up to see whether you were all right. I didn't touch you."

"Was it you who folded my clothes?"

"Yes. I picked them up and folded them. Then I went back to my room and waited for you to leave. When you walked down the street, you looked okay."

"Let me get this straight. You sat in your room while five guys raped me. You came upstairs and folded my clothes. You watched me leave. And then you stalked me for the next five months." Galina's whole body shook with rage.

"I guess I felt responsible. I should have tried to stop them."

"You're damn right you should have! But you didn't. And you didn't report them. And afterwards you kept on living with those guys. You didn't do one damn thing but follow me around campus. For God's sake, why?"

"To make amends. I didn't know what else to do."

Galina pulled her right arm back and squeezed her hand into a tight fist. There flashed in Steve's eyes a recognition of what was about to happen, but he made no effort to avoid the blow. The heel of her palm smashed into his face. A popping sound. Steve took it in silence and stood before her, blood pouring from his nose.

"Give me their names," she said. "If you want to make amends, that's the first thing you can do." She thrust her clipboard at him. "Write down their names."

Blood dribbled onto the sheet of paper as he wrote. His nose was bent to one side, and he was crying. The sight of his tears revolted her. Galina wanted to hit him again.

"Here," he said. She glanced at the list.

"Your name too. Sign it at the bottom. Date it. Write down your phone number and the address."

He did as she asked. No questions. No protest.

"It's not over yet," she said. Then she released him.

When she got back to her room, Galina read the list, saying each name aloud. She could not see their faces as she read, but she could picture five young men being loaded into a police van, led into the city jail, locked in cells. In her mind she saw them handcuffed in a courtroom. She saw their mothers weeping—their fathers too. For the first time in months, Galina felt good about something. She folded the sheet of paper and put it into her desk drawer.

Galina kept the good feeling with her all through exams. She attacked her books with vengeful energy. It was part of her revenge to do better than she had ever done before, despite the rape, despite being seven months pregnant. She thought of Hamlet's vow to sweep to his revenge "with wings as swift as meditation or the thoughts of love." Well, Galina would waddle like a duck to her revenge, but it would be just as sweet.

Mavis and Paula finished their finals two days before Galina. She was sitting at her desk reviewing her lecture notes on *Samson Agonistes* when they knocked on her door.

"Come in," she called.

They didn't sit. Galina didn't stand.

"How are you feeling?" Mavis asked.

"Like a stranded whale. Six more weeks."

"You're looking good. How's your blood pressure?"

"It's okay. The nurse at Health Services says it is."

There was an awkward pause. Paula, moving toward the door, said, "Well, good luck. See you in the fall?" Her voice rose, making it a question.

"No. I won't come back here. Most likely I'll transfer to McMaster so I can live at home. Mom can help with the babysitting."

"You're lucky," said Paula. "My mother wouldn't do that for me."

"She doesn't know yet. But she's a Catholic. She'll think I'm some kind of saint because I didn't have an abortion. Anyway, that's what I hope."

Mavis patted Galina's shoulder. "Keep in touch."

Two days later, Galina wrote her last exam. When she had handed in her paper, she went back to her room. Time to pack. Empty cartons received her books, her binders, her laptop. A caretaker brought her trunk up from the basement, and into it went Galina's clothes—not the shapeless bargain-store dresses, but the clothes she had worn before her troubles began.

Then Galina got out of the dress she was wearing. She undid the buttons, pulled it up over her head, and let it drop. It lay on the floor, crumpled, discarded, consigned to the garbage along with the rest of her other oversized dresses.

Upon her bed sat a large, flattish cardboard box that displayed in elegant script the words "Lady in Waiting." Galina opened the box, broke the paper seal that fastened the tissue paper inside, and drew out a two-piece linen dress, faultlessly elegant and sewn with exquisite detail. The colour was cream, with dark green trim. It was a maternity dress, obviously, but in a style that Lady Diana might have chosen—perfect for a young woman on a mission.

The time had come. Galina dressed carefully. She made up her face, brushed her hair, put on her pearl-drop earrings. The last thing she did was to tuck the bloodstained paper with the six names into her handbag.

"This is for you, baby." She patted her belly as she left the dorm with a No Frills plastic shopping bag on her arm. On her way to Earl Street she picked up eight empty beer bottles from the front lawns of houses in the student ghetto.

The house on Earl Street had not changed. The broken-down sofa was on the porch. The bicycles were chained to the railings. So the students had not left. Good. She had counted on them sticking around to party after their exams.

On the lawn lay four more beer bottles to add to her collection. She lined up all twelve in a neat row on the sidewalk.

The first she hurled through the living room window. There was a wonderful smash as the glass shattered. She aimed the next bottle at a second storey window. It missed, but she hit it on the second try. Then she sent a bottle crashing through the window next to it. Now warmed up, Galina had eight bottles left.

The third storey window was a long way up. A long way, and the branches of the maple tree, with its budding twigs, shielded the glass. It took her all eight bottles to break that window. But she got it. Her last bottle smashed through just as the police arrived.

The officer who arrested her looked flabbergasted. A pregnant girl, fashionably dressed and perfectly sober, hurling beer bottles through windows! Galina explained nothing, made no excuses. She thanked the officer who helped her into the back seat of the police car. On the way to the police station, she held on her lap the handbag that contained the piece of paper with the names.

The Darkness of Her Flames

The mail slot cover snapped shut. At the sound of letters splattering onto the slate floor, Ruth marked her place in *Love's Desire* and set it on the coffee table. The romantic entanglements of Celestica Jones must wait until another time. Today might bring a letter from Charles.

Ruth got up from the sofa but did not leave the living room until she had given the mail carrier half a minute to get down the porch steps and out to the sidewalk. Better not rush. If he were to glance back and see her through the sidelight by the front door, he might think that she was one of those women who have nothing better to do than sit around waiting for the post every afternoon.

Today's mail brought no letter from Charles. All the envelopes lying under the mail slot looked like bills and begging letters. Disappointing, but not surprising. The letter she expected had been mailed on Friday. This was Monday. Since it hadn't arrived today, it would tomorrow. So she still had something to look forward to; for in love, anticipation heightens the sweet fulfillment of desire.

Ruth picked up the envelopes, took them upstairs to her bedroom, and sat down at her desk.

On Ruth's desk, unanswered letters were stacked in one pile, unpaid bills in another. Her paper knife and pens rested on a small enamelled tray. Her desk was white with gold trim—French Provincial—small and pretty. Bob couldn't have got his fat knees under it even if he had wanted to. But of course he didn't, and that was just as well.

Across the room stood Ruth's dressing table, with her gilt jewellery box in the centre, flanked by a crystal bowl of pot-pourri on one side, perfume bottles on the other. A dainty lamp with a fluted silk shade was placed at either end.

On her queen-sized bed—she thought of it as hers—silk pillows coordinated with the pale green shot-taffeta duvet cover. Ruth's room enclosed her pleasantly. Charming and romantic, like herself.

Ruth picked up her paper knife. It too was pretty—Toledo steel, shaped like a small dagger with a five-inch stiletto blade. The haft was emblazoned with Moorish designs.

She slit open the bills, placed them in their proper pile, and then turned to the begging letters. The first appeal was from the SPCA. "Fight Puppy Mills!" it urged. Ruth snorted as she tossed it into the waste paper basket. Tiresome requests from Grace Hospital and the Kidney Foundation met the same fate.

Ruth's fingers drummed on the desk as she considered how to get through the next twenty-four hours. A pity that Charles' letter hadn't come today. His last one had been destroyed too hastily, torn into bits and flushed down the toilet before she knew the words by heart. That was Bob's fault. His unexpected arrival had thrown her into panic. At the sound of his voice, "Honey, I'm home!" she had leapt from the bed with Charles' letter in her hand and fled into the bathroom.

Normally, Ruth got rid of Charles' letters as soon as she had them memorized. It would be a disaster if one ever fell into Bob's hands. How could she possibly explain?

And it wasn't just Bob finding one that worried her. Tara—Tara the Terrible, as Bob and Ruth had aptly nick-named her at the age of four—was the real problem. Tara snooped. She pawed through Ruth's closet, tried on her jewellery, read her mail. Ruth had evidence of this. She set traps, such as leaving a paper clip in a strategic position on top of a letter so that she would know if it had been moved. Of course, Charles' letters were never in the pile on Ruth's desk. His stayed hidden until they were destroyed.

Tara slammed into the house and stormed into the kitchen. Ruth, peeling potatoes at the sink, looked at her daughter. No longer did the spectacle of Tara's multiple piercings make her flinch. Unlike Bob, who threatened to remove Tara's hardware with a wire cutter, Ruth had grown indifferent to the rings, studs and bolts that penetrated eyebrow, ears, nose and navel. She had even got used to the belly-baring jeans that scarcely covered Tara's pubic bone.

"Tara, did you hang up your coat? I don't want snow melting all over the floor."

Tara growled something monosyllabic as she opened the fridge door. When she bent over to take out a Coke, two inches of bum crack showed over the top of her jeans. The spectacle made Ruth wince. Why did Tara think it attractive to expose so much? Her big butt was hardly her best feature. Too bad she didn't take after Ruth's side of the family.

"I wouldn't wear those pants so low," Ruth said smugly. "When you bend over, it looks like your bum is ready to pop out."

"How I wear my clothes is my business." Glowering ferociously, Tara stomped up the stairs to her bedroom.

Ruth dropped the potato she had been peeling and set her paring knife on the counter. Why did Tara *want* to dress like that—the piercings, the clothes that revealed just about everything? Rebellion, maybe? Anger at Bob for being away so much? Anger at Ruth for setting a standard that Tara couldn't hope to reach? Rebellion was normal. Ruth had rebelled when she was fourteen—smoked pot, got drunk on lemon gin. But she had never done anything that would damage her reputation or attract the wrong kind of boyfriend.

Bob had asked her once, when they first started dating, "What do you want from life?" She had answered, "To be safe." He had looked astonished, as if so simple a goal were beyond comprehension. "What about you?" she had asked.

And he had said, "I want to be rich."

Well, that had suited her. Bob would make the money; she would make the perfect home.

Ruth picked up the potato, carved out the eyes and those ugly pale sprouts.

Problem was, Bob never did get rich. Comfortable, but not rich. He worked like a dog, travelling all over setting up those Burger Master franchises, while she, safe in her pretty home, chose wallpaper, read romances, and dreamed about Charles.

Ruth peeled another potato while listening to Tara's feet clump overhead. In a few minutes the air began to thud and the ceiling shake with the beat of Tara's music, if you could call it that. Her head ached by the time she had finished peeling.

The clumping stopped. That might mean Tara was sprawled on her bed talking on the phone. The timing was right. Tara always phoned her best friend, Heather, as soon as she got home from school.

After placing the potatoes in a saucepan of water, Ruth tiptoed to the phone on the kitchen wall. Covering the mouthpiece with a dishcloth, she lifted the receiver. First time lucky. The conversation was underway.

Ruth recognized Heather's cheerful, girlish voice. "My mom never says anything when we go up to my room. One time she asked if we were being responsible. I said we always were. After that she left me alone."

"You are *so* lucky!" Tara answered. "My mom never leaves us alone. Last week she knocked on my door to ask if

Tony and me wanted some potato chips. Me with my panties around my ankles. Christ, I could have killed her."

"So why don't you go to Tony's place?"

Ruth's hand trembled as she hung up the phone. The little fool! Sex, sex, sex. That's all teenagers thought about. Did Tara think sex would make her happy? Ruth could tell her a thing or two. Handsome Tony with his gleaming eyes—in twenty years his smooth brown arms would be like a pair of hams, his chest would be covered with a mat of hair, and his belly would stick out so far he wouldn't be able to see his cock when he stood up.

Like Bob.

She grimaced at the thought of Bob naked. The way he climbed on top of her, grunting like a hog. His sweaty, heavy body pinning her down. The only good thing about sex with Bob was its scarcity. If he weren't away most of the time, setting up Burger Master franchises all over the country, she'd have to cope with it every week, every night if he had his way.

Love with Charles was altogether different. "A woman's most important erogenous zone is her mind," was what he had written in one of his marvellous letters. So expressive! But then, Charles was an artist.

Another letter arrived the next day. Ruth snatched up the creamy, vellum envelope that was his trademark, leaving the bills and junk mail on the hall floor. It was all she could do not to rip the letter open on the spot. But no, a love letter, like love itself, should not be rushed.

Pinching the corner of the envelope between her forefinger and thumb, she carried it to her bedroom and sat at her desk. She picked up her paper knife and with one deft motion sliced the envelope open. Ruth unfolded the letter, gazed with admiration at the elegant calligraphy that required such care to write, and began to read:

Dearest Ruth,

Last night I dreamed that you lay next to me, with your red-gold hair spread loose upon the pillow. Your lips, half parted, sighed my name. Your breath smelled like violets. When I kissed your cheek, you opened your eyes and smiled.

My precious one, when I dream of the moonlight in your eyes, the stars of heaven whirl inside my fevered brain. Oh, let me burn in the darkness of your flames.

Your own forever,
Charles

She read it again, lingering as she whispered the final sentence: "Oh, let me burn in the darkness of your flames." Ruth raised her eyes to the reflection in the gilt-edged mirror over her desk. She arched her brows and parted her lips. "You're hot," she purred. "Like fire!"

Downstairs, the front door opened. Ruth glanced at her watch. Christ! Four o'clock already. She put down the letter, piled half a dozen bills on top, and got up so fast she knocked over her chair.

She heard Tara's voice, then Tony's. Two sets of feet on the stairs.

"Oh, no you don't," she muttered. It was time these hormone-raddled adolescents stopped using her home as a free motel. Standing at the top of the stairs, arms folded across her chest, she confronted them as they reached the landing.

"Where are you two going?"

"To my room to listen to CDs." Tara stared coldly at her mother.

"You can listen to CDs in the family room."

"The bedroom's better."

"Better for what?"

Tara glared.

"C'mon, Tony, let's get out of here." With a toss of her head, Tara turned about and marched down the stairs. Tony paused. When his eyes met Ruth's, she felt her knees go weak. His light brown eyes shone like a cat's, luminous but utterly without depth. His hair was glossy, and it fit close to his skull in a way that reminded her of a smooth-furred animal, something swift and fierce.

He ducked his head toward Ruth in a deep nod that was almost a bow and licked his upper lip, then turned and followed Tara down the stairs.

Ruth watched him put on his coat with a supple movement. No boy of seventeen should have a body so lithe and sensual. He turned his head sharply while opening the door, and looked at Ruth with an easy smile, as if they were confederates.

After Tara and Tony had left, Ruth went into the living

room and sat down. She felt her blood run hot to think of how he had looked at her and licked his lip. She recognized the invitation.

What did he see when he looked at her? An unsatisfied middle-aged woman who would be easy prey? How dare he! There was nothing middle-aged about her. Flat stomach. Slender, shapely legs. Working out at the gym five times a week kept her body as trim as a twenty year old's. And although the red-gold tints in her hair now came from a bottle, at forty she was a handsome woman.

Tara, who took after Bob's side of the family, would not age as well. Already lumpish at fourteen, how had she managed to attract a boy like Tony?

At bedtime Ruth discovered that Charles' letter had disappeared. It wasn't under the bills that she had tossed on top that afternoon. It was nowhere on her desk. She pulled the desk out from the wall to see whether it might have slipped down behind. No letter.

Tara had taken it, beyond a doubt. While Ruth relaxed in her bath, face coated with exfoliating mask, Tara had been snooping. Why the hell didn't I hide it somewhere? Ruth fumed. How could she have been so careless?

Ruth sat down at her desk. One last time she riffled through the bills and unanswered correspondence, knowing the letter was not there. She put her hand to her brow; her head was pounding.

What would Tara do with the letter? That was the key question. She might show it to her friends, pass it around amidst a chorus of giggles and guffaws. It was easy to imagine the mockery, the hilarity in their voices as they read Charles' tender, passionate words.

After she had shown it to her friends, would Tara give it to her father? The thought of Bob reading Charles' letter made Ruth's stomach clench into a hard knot.

Blackmail was a third possibility. Tara might try to blackmail her own mother; she was capable of that. The letter gave her power. She could ask for clothes, money, and special privileges. Ruth would be unable to refuse.

What am I going to do? Ruth asked herself. She could drag Tara out of bed and demand the letter back. Or she could wait for Tara to make the first move. That might be smarter. If you didn't know what to do, better do nothing at all.

The next afternoon at four o'clock the front door opened and Tara came in. Tony wasn't with her. Thank God! Ruth, not moving from her spot on the sofa, heard Tara clunk along the hall to the kitchen, rummage in the cupboard and get something from the fridge. What would Tara do next? Would she say anything about the letter?

Tara wandered into the living room with a bowl of nachos and a Coke. She stood in front of Ruth.

"Have a nice afternoon?" Tara smirked.

"Nothing out of the ordinary."

"Anybody come over?"

That was a sly smile! Sly, and easy to interpret. Tara was imagining her mother wrapped in a lover's embrace. An afternoon of debauchery and fornication. Yet what could

Ruth say? Explanation would make matters worse.

"No," said Ruth, "nobody came over."

"Did you go out?"

"No."

"Ha!" Tara marched up the stairs to her room.

Ruth went into the kitchen to make a cup of tea. Her hands shook as she poured the water into the kettle. As it was coming to the boil, the phone rang. She picked up the receiver. Bob calling from Timmins. He would be home the next day.

"Tomorrow! That's awfully soon."

"The franchisee had the cash. We got the agreement hammered out pretty fast. Anyway, I'll be home tomorrow evening."

"You're going to drive all the way from Timmins in one day? In the middle of winter?" Ruth heard her voice becoming hysterical. Bob must not come home until the letter had been dealt with.

"I drove up here in one day, didn't I? What's the big deal? Something wrong?"

She took a quick breath. "No. Everything's fine. Drive carefully."

Ruth put a tea bag into a mug and poured in boiling water. How could she get the letter back? Damn Tara! Ruth stabbed the tea bag with her spoon. The spoon was a knife, and the teabag was Tara. She stabbed the tea bag again. What had she ever done to deserve such a daughter?

Ruth pulled the broken tea bag from the mug, dropped it into the sink, and returned to the living room with her mug of tea shaking in her hand. It sloshed over the rim as she sat down on the sofa. Ruth drank her tea, filtering out the leaves between her front teeth, while she contemplated the worst: divorce.

Not that she dreaded the prospect of Bob disappearing from her life. For a long time, her marriage had been a loveless habit. Bob was a presence in the house, like the refrigerator. No, more like the vacuum cleaner, which she took out of the closet once a week.

What Ruth dreaded was the spectre of going back to work. No more mornings in the gym. No more quiet afternoons reading romances and waiting for the mail. Christ! She hadn't had a job for years. She would have to re-qualify as a nurse. And when she did, she'd be back where she had started half a lifetime ago: charts, overcrowded wards, and twelve-hour shifts. She had already endured more than her share of arrogant doctors, complaining patients and sore feet.

After work, when she got home, Tara would be there. Ruth would be a single parent, and she simply couldn't face it. Tara, with her hardware and her perpetual scowl, could live with Bob. Ruth would let him have custody. But Bob was out of town most of the time, so that wasn't going to work.

Loveless or not, Ruth's marriage was the foundation of her life. And her life, despite its flaws, suited her very well. For romance, she had Charles. As for Bob, there was a kind of martyrdom in devoting her life to a husband she secretly disliked.

Up in her room, directly overhead, Tara had put on a CD. The music pounded through the ceiling. It shook the house.

Ruth felt a headache coming on.

She lay down on the sofa and pressed one ear against the seat while holding a cushion over the other. She would lie here for five minutes, then go up to Tara's room and demand the letter.

Five minutes became ten minutes, then fifteen, then an hour. It was time to start supper, but Ruth did not move.

At eight o'clock Tara went out. Ruth didn't care where she was going. Probably to meet Tony. Maybe, if she left Tara alone, she could forget about the letter. Wait and see. Perhaps nothing would happen at all.

The living room faced east—a feature that Ruth had always liked, for she loved the morning sunshine that slanted through the bay windows, casting red, green and blue ribbons of light through the bevelled glass, as if through prisms, upon the beige carpet.

She sat on the sofa drinking a second coffee, as she usually did after Tara had left for school. The living room possessed a lovely ambience for reading Charles' letters, though of course she no longer had one to read. She tried to remember the best parts of the most recent one: "Your breath smelled like violets … the stars of heaven whirl … let me burn in the darkness of your flames."

Although still beautiful, the words had lost their power to carry her away. Hard reality weighed her down. Tonight Bob would be home.

Ruth glanced at her watch. Aerobic dancing this morning. Time to get ready. She was sipping the last of her coffee when the doorbell rang. Automatically she stood up and headed towards the hall. Apprehension came over her even before she saw that the person at the door was Tony.

He wore a leather bomber jacket and no hat. His glossy black hair was frosted with snow.

Ruth hesitated. Really, there was no reason why she shouldn't open the door and find out what he wanted. She couldn't just stand there staring at him. She turned the knob. As Tony entered, a gust of snow came with him.

"Cold day," she said.

"That depends." The corner of his mouth lifted. Why should her bland comment on the weather elicit this response? Ruth stepped back.

"Tara's not here."

"I know. She's at school." He took off his jacket and handed it to her. Taken aback by his self-assurance, she didn't ask why he wasn't at school as well. Did he notice that her hands trembled as she hung his jacket in the closet?

She turned to face him. The silence in the house was complete, but there was a drumming in her ears that got louder and louder. His eyes looked yellow in the morning light. Now she recognized what they were like—the gemstone, tiger's eye.

"What do you want?" she asked.

He fumbled in the pocket of his jeans, pulled out a cream-coloured envelope. His mouth turned up in a tight smile.

"I want to burn in the darkness of your flames."

"Where did you get that?" She lunged for the letter, but

he raised it over her head like a man offering a biscuit to a dog. The dog must beg.

"Tara gave it to me. Said she found it on your desk. Come and get it if you want it." With a turn of his head, he motioned toward the staircase.

She grabbed for the letter again. He moved backward, stepped up onto the first tread, then the second. Ruth followed, step by step. At the turn of the landing she made another try. Physically, he was not big, scarcely taller than her own five-foot-seven frame. But he seemed to be concentrated, to have the strength of two men packed into his body. He grasped her wrist and hauled her the rest of the way upstairs.

As he dragged her into the bedroom, the letter fell from his hand. From the corner of her eye she saw the cream-coloured rectangle lying on the pale carpet. Gripping her shoulders, he propelled her backwards inch by inch. She felt the hard edge of her desk against the top of her thighs. He bent her backwards, leaning over her. He was kissing her throat with fierce kisses. She smelled his sweat, felt his breath on her cheek. As his body pressed her body, a shudder passed through her loins. In a moment her bones would melt.

"Stop!"

"Relax, Mommy! You've been asking for this. Let's see if you can fuck as good as Tara."

Good God! Mother and daughter! He couldn't get away with this. Every muscle of her body stiffened. He was strong, but she had strength too.

Ruth's right hand was free. Her paper knife was in the enamelled tray on her desk. Her fingers brushed aside a sheaf of papers and closed upon the haft. She knew where to aim.

She struck hard. The stiletto point punched through his clothing, through his skin, into the firm mass of his body. The knife entered under his ribs, pushed upward toward his lungs. She didn't hear him cry out; she couldn't hear anything above the roar of blood inside her head. It took all her strength, everything she had, to force that blade in.

Their eyes met. What she saw in his eyes was shock, not fear. He gave a kind of grunt. His body was still half upon hers, their faces inches apart.

"What the fuck have you done?"

"What have I done?" She heard herself speaking as if from far away. "I believe that I have pierced your descending aorta." She pushed him off her, wrenching the knife from his body as he slumped to the floor.

The blood spurted, torrents of red blood spreading over the pale carpet.

"Call 911," he begged. "Get an ambulance."

"Yes." She moved as if in a trance along the upstairs hall to the telephone table, but by the time she reached it, her mind was clear. Without help, he would be dead in fifteen minutes. She picked up the receiver but did not touch the buttons. "We need an ambulance. There's been an accident. 940 Dovecote Drive. Yes. Yes." She gave her phone number, and then returned to the bedroom.

He lay on his side. "When will the ambulance …?" Shudders ran through his body.

"You don't have long to wait." Ruth sat down on the edge of the bed. Many years had passed since she last watched someone die. It took ten minutes, maybe less, for the light to fade from his eyes until they were nothing but a pair of stones.

Then she picked up Charles' letter from the pool of dark blood where it lay. She carried it into the bathroom, tore the letter and the envelope into tiny pieces, and dropped them into the toilet bowl. Not all the bits disappeared with the first flush. She flushed again, and when the water's swirl had calmed, not a scrap of Charles' beautiful stationery remained. Ruth gave one last tender glance into the toilet bowl.

"Goodbye, Charles. My sweet, my precious. My perfect lover."

Now was the time to call 911. First the ambulance would come, then the police. She supposed that somebody would fetch Tara from school. By the time Bob got home, there would be police tape around the house. Ruth had her story ready: Tara's boyfriend had tried to rape her. His death was self-defence. Bob would buy that too.

What about the letter? Well, it was gone, never to be produced as evidence of anything. Maybe it never existed.

Still, before she made the call to 911, it would be wise to get rid of her half-empty box of cream-coloured stationery and her calligraphy pen.

A Wanton Disregard

Bill's cellphone rang. Damn! Vera again. Every two minutes for the last twenty! So what the hell was he supposed to do? He was already ten klicks over the limit, racing down Wyandotte Avenue.

He wouldn't answer, that's what. But the phone kept on ringing, and he answered it. He always did.

"Vera, can't you keep him happy for twenty minutes?"

"Mr. Sugarman's already been waiting twenty minutes. He was on time. You weren't."

"Make him a coffee."

"I've done that."

"Tell him it isn't my fault. I got held up at my last meeting. The client was late."

"He says if you're not here in ten minutes, his business

goes elsewhere."

"Oh shit!" Bill swerved the car around a jaywalker. "Vera, you still there?"

"Yeah."

"Tell him ten minutes." Ten minutes to get back, or a million-dollar contract goes down the sewer.

Bill floored the accelerator.

That's when he felt the bump. Felt it. Saw nothing, until all at once a man's face looked in through the windshield. Eyes wide, staring into his. Mouth open. A hand waving. No, it was clutching air. Bill braked as the man rolled off the hood.

Screams on all sides. A woman shrieked, "The little boy's under the car!"

Bill opened the car door and swung his legs around to get out. His knees buckled, and he had to hang on to the door frame to steady himself. All the air had been sucked out of his lungs.

When he looked down, he saw a small white sneaker, a blue sock, a plump leg that twitched and then lay still. Shiny drops of blood, bright as paint, lay splattered on the asphalt.

Twenty feet away, the man who had stared at Bill through the windshield lay motionless on the pavement, his eyes still wide open.

Bill sat down heavily on the car seat. He lowered his face into his hands. "What have I done?" He groaned. "What have I done?"

The framed picture that Lydia Carey kept on her bedside table was the first thing she saw every morning and the last thing she saw at night. It was there to help her remember the faces of her husband and child, and also to remind her that the price for their deaths had not been paid.

Lydia had taken the photograph in the backyard, a week before they died. Matthew and Mattie: father and son. Mattie is sitting on Matthew's shoulders. His hands rest on either side of his daddy's throat, plump little fingers spread wide. He is looking down into Matthew's face. Matthew, his head half turned, is looking up at his son. Their smiles are of perfect trust and love. Matthew is holding on to Mattie's legs just above his ankles. On the boy's feet are new white sneakers and blue socks.

Lydia had been in Mattie's room making the bed when two officers, a man and a woman, brought the news. The police-woman was black. She held tight to Lydia's hands. Lydia remembered her compassionate eyes, her warm West Indian voice and the strength that flowed from her hands.

The next-door neighbour came over. She made tea, phoned relatives and stayed until the living room began to fill with people. Lydia's sister Diane was there. So were Lydia's mom and dad, and Matthew's parents and his two brothers. People lined the walls, sitting on the sofa, in the armchairs, on chairs brought in from the dining room and kitchen. The only clear space was the corner to the right of the fireplace where Lydia sat, her hands clutched on her lap, holding a sodden handkerchief. Her eyes were hot, her head pounded, and everything was a blur. Somebody gave her a pill. Diane told her to go upstairs and lie down.

For no special reason, she went into Mattie's room, and found there a deep calm, despite the sound of voices from downstairs. She lay down on the half-made bed and hugged Mattie's pillow. His sheets smelled sweetly of soap and milk, mingled with a whiff of urine from the plastic mattress cover.

Stick-on stars twinkled on Mattie's bedroom ceiling. Ponies pranced, bears danced and circus clowns juggled on the walls. The floor was a jumble of toys. Silent drum. Oversized Lego for tiny fingers. A teddy bear flat on its back stared up at the starry sky.

Voices floated up. Frequently someone spoke her name, but she didn't care. After a while she got off the bed and sat on the floor amidst the toys. She picked up the teddy bear and held it on her lap while her mind struggled with vague and peculiar thoughts. She imagined that Mattie was hiding in the closet, and she squeezed her eyes shut.

"One, two, three. Ready or not! Here I come." She listened for his little boy giggle. "Mattie! Where are you?"

The day after the funeral, everyone left except Diane.

"You don't have to stay," said Lydia. "I'm fine."

"Sure you are. But my kids are at school all day. Joe can look after things for a couple of weeks. So don't argue."

Argue with Diane? What would be the point? From as far back as Lydia could remember, Diane always won. And so she took over, filling the house with her bulky presence and with the sweet, comfortable smell of muffins and fresh-baked bread. Diane forced Lydia to eat. She watered plants, vacuumed, answered the phone. For the first few days she didn't talk too much; Lydia was grateful for that.

It was okay having her around as long as she didn't mind sleeping on the living room sofa. But after a week she started complaining that her back hurt. She needed a bed.

When Lydia didn't get the hint, Diane came right out and asked: "Will it be all right if I sleep in Mattie's room?"

Lydia pretended not to hear.

"Well, how about it?"

"Mattie's room?" Lydia started to sweat. "I don't think so."

"Why not?"

"Mattie's room should stay the way it is."

Diane put her arm around Lydia. "Honey, you can't make his room into a shrine. Denial makes things worse. You have to let go."

Lydia straightened her shoulders, took a deep breath, and held her body stiff against Diane's encircling arm. Denial was her only defense. How could she let it go?

"Listen to me," Diane said. "Grieving is a process. First there's shock. Then denial. That's where you are now. These are normal stages you have to go through in order to reach acceptance. You can't let yourself get stuck along the way."

"I don't believe it." Lydia spoke fiercely, for the thought of acceptance repelled her.

But Diane's insistent voice bombarded her with logic. Through habit and fatigue, she caved in.

"I guess you're right," Lydia said.

"Of course I am." Diane gave Lydia's shoulder a squeeze and let her go.

"Take Mattie's room. I'll change the sheets and pick up his toys."

"I can do that."

"No, I want to."

Lydia stripped off Mattie's sheets, took off the mattress cover and made up the bed. She returned the toys to the toy box and the teddy bear to its place on the shelf. When she had finished, the room did look more welcoming. And it was still Mattie's room, his to claim as soon as Diane left.

That evening Lydia helped Diane cook dinner. Afterwards they made popcorn and watched TV the way they used to do when they were kids. Every minute, Lydia felt Diane's critical, appraising eyes upon her. All things considered, Lydia put on a good act.

"I'm going to be fine," she said as she clicked off the remote after the late news. "I can cope."

"I'll stay a few more days." Diane picked up the empty popcorn bowls to take them to the kitchen. "One thing we have to do is get some cartons from the supermarket so we can pack Matthew's clothes."

"What for?" Lydia's stomach clenched.

"To take to the Salvation Army."

"Not Matthew's clothes." She turned swiftly towards her sister, feeling the blood rise to her face. On this she would not yield.

"Sorry," said Diane. "I didn't mean to upset you. You're bound to feel anger. I guess you're reaching that stage."

Lydia felt hostile, yet spoke gravely, as if to a stranger. "You know I don't believe that stuff. It's too mechanical, as if people were robots."

"Yeah, well, it does happen."

"Not for me."

The next day, at dinnertime, Joe phoned. He and the boys needed Diane. They had run out of clean underwear and the house was a mess.

"You'd think a grown man could manage a house and a couple of kids for a few weeks," she said with a touch of smugness.

"They miss you. Go home and take care of them."

"I guess I should." Diane shifted uncomfortably, as if she had something awkward to say. "If you don't mind me asking, are you okay for money?"

Lydia did mind, but answered calmly, "More than okay."

"Are you sure? Because if you need …"

"Don't worry. Matthew had mortgage insurance and life insurance. Two hundred thousand." She paused. "Double for accidental death."

Diane's eyes widened. "That's a good bit of money."

"It takes off the pressure."

Lydia stood up abruptly to show that the subject was closed and put on the kettle for tea. "Now I have a question for you."

"Sure."

"Tell me about the man who drove the car."

When Diane didn't answer, Lydia turned around to face her. Diane was staring at some invisible spot on the wall. "You mustn't think about him. It interferes with …"

Lydia interrupted. "I don't want to hear about the grieving process. Just tell me about the man who drove the car. I have a right to know."

"Dwelling on it won't help you in the slightest."

"Tell me."

"I just know what was in the newspaper."

"I wasn't reading the newspapers."

Diane turned her eyes towards Lydia. "His name is William Shaw, known as Bill, and he's a sales rep for a developer."

"I want personal stuff."

"He's thirty-six. Married. Coaches kids' hockey."

"So he has children." Lydia kept her voice casual as she lifted the teapot from its shelf.

"I guess so."

"Boys? Girls? How old?"

"I'm not sure."

"Don't tell me you don't know."

"Okay." Diane sighed. "He has a ten-year-old girl who plays hockey for the Riverbank Mosquitoes. And another girl in kindergarten."

"Thanks." That was what Lydia needed to know.

During breakfast they reminisced about family vacations and childhood pets. Lydia kept up a stream of small talk, avoiding any topic that might cause Diane to lengthen her stay.

"Joe and the kids will be happy to get you back," she said as she started to clear the table.

"Yeah. Clean underwear and real food. Even kids get tired of pizza."

"You better get packed if you want to be home in time to cook supper."

Diane glanced at the kitchen wall clock. Nine-thirty. She stood up, carrying her coffee. "You're right. I should be on the road by ten."

Lydia listened to Diane's footsteps overhead. Ten more minutes. Five more minutes. The toilet flushed. One more minute.

At ten on the button, Diane came downstairs. Lydia walked her out to the car and waved good-bye. When Diane's car had disappeared around the corner, Lydia went inside. She closed the front door and leaned against it, listening to the silence.

After a few minutes, a car approached. It stopped outside, and the car door slammed. Christ! Had Diane come back? Lydia held her breath until silence returned, then tiptoed up the stairs to the bedroom that had been hers and Matthew's.

Matthew had his own closet off the master bedroom, and Lydia had hers. That was a feature Lydia loved about this house: two big walk-in closets. Since Matthew's death, she had avoided entering his. Once or twice she had gone in to hang something up, but left in haste.

Now, as she stood in front of the closed closet door, a feeling came over her that Matthew was very near. Not his spirit. This was physical. As her right hand turned the door-knob, her left strayed towards the light switch, then drew back. She slipped inside and shut the door behind her.

In the darkness and warmth, she inhaled the smell of Matthew: his sweat, his aftershave. She hugged his clothes, rubbed her cheeks against the rough tweed of his jacket, ran her hands up and down his jeans. Burrowing into the fleece of his sheepskin coat, she almost felt his body touching hers.

Then the telephone rang, and the illusion was gone. Lydia raised her head. Maybe Diane was calling from out on the highway. Flat tire. Breakdown. Accident. Yes, she must answer the phone.

Light rushed in as Lydia opened the closet door. She stumbled around to the far side of the bed, where the phone sat on Matthew's bedside table.

"Hello?"

A woman's voice, but not Diane's. Lydia recognized the West Indian tones.

"Good morning, Mrs. Carey. I'm Staff Sergeant Wallace at the Central Police Station. Constable Burns and I …"

"Yes. I remember you."

"I'm calling to tell you that I'm assigned as your contact person."

"Contact person?"

"I'm the officer who'll keep in touch with you through the court process."

"You mean through the trial?"

"There'll be no trial. Mr. Shaw is pleading guilty. With twenty witnesses watching him run the red light, plus his own statement after the accident, he thought he might as well get the whole thing over. The only question that remains is the sentence."

"How long will he be in jail?"

"That's up to the judge. All sorts of factors affect sentencing."

"In a case like this, what would be normal?"

"For Criminal Negligence Causing Death, maybe one year."

Lydia sat in Number One Courtroom beside Diane, who had returned to lend sisterly support. Bill Shaw, behind Plexiglas in the prisoner's box, wore a dark grey suit, blue shirt, and striped maroon and grey tie. Shouldn't he be wearing drab prison clothes? It was all wrong for him to look well-dressed, his sandy hair neatly combed.

He sat with his arms folded across his chest, as if he were trying to hold in his feelings. Once or twice his eyes scanned the watching public, but most of the time he was looking at his wife, an olive-skinned woman with darkly arched brows and a long nose, who constantly dabbed her eyes with a tissue. She wore a blue maternity dress with a pleated front.

"Did you know she was pregnant?" Diane whispered.

"No."

"Looks about seven months."

"Six or seven."

"I feel sorry for her."

"I don't."

"It would be horrible to give birth while your husband was in jail."

"I couldn't care less."

Lydia read her victim impact statement to the Court. As she read, she had the feeling that the statement was about someone else, though every word was true. She had lost her husband's love and companionship. She had lost the joy of caring for her child and of watching him grow to manhood. Her desolation at having both husband and child snatched from her was complete and irremediable.

As she finished, Lydia stared straight at Bill Shaw. His face had turned pale. When her eyes met his, he turned his head away.

When Lydia returned to her seat, she saw that Mrs. Shaw had given up dabbing her eyes with her tissue. Sobbing noisily, she let the tears roll down her cheeks. Pregnancy does that, Lydia thought, makes women broody and tender-hearted.

Suddenly Mrs. Shaw stopped sobbing. A look of wonder crossed her face as she placed her hand on her abdomen. Lydia understood. She remembered the feeling, that soft pummelling from inside, the bumping of a tiny knee or shoulder. It wasn't fair! Why should Bill Shaw's wife have this baby, and she no child at all?

Diane grabbed her arm. "Get a grip," she whispered.

"What?"

"You're crying."

Lydia blew her nose and sat up stiffly.

The defence attorney described his client's contrition. How those six seconds had changed his life. How he would never forgive himself.

The judge appeared unmoved. "Individual deterrence is not the only issue," he said, looking at his notes. "I don't expect this particular offender to appear in court again on a similar charge. But the public has to get the message. Conduct that shows a wanton disregard for the lives or safety of other persons must be criminally punished. He was driving fifteen kilometres over the speed limit while talking on his cellphone. He ran a red light and killed two people."

Bill Shaw got fourteen months imprisonment and a three-year driving suspension.

His lawyer asked the Court to recommend admission to the temporary absence program so that the convicted man could continue his employment, for he was married with two young children and a third on the way.

The judge shook his head. "General deterrence must be considered in a case like this. A custodial sentence is required."

Back at the house, Lydia threw her coat on the sofa and went straight for the liquor cabinet. She pulled out a bottle of scotch. "I need this."

"When did you start drinking?"

"Today. Right now."

"Put the bottle away," Diane said. "I'll make a pot of tea and we can talk."

"What's there to talk about? Shaw got fourteen months."
She poured herself a drink and gulped it down.

"You think it should be more?"

"Fourteen years," she said viciously.

"Well, that's not going to happen."

"That's the problem." Lydia poured another drink. She waved the bottle at Diane. "Sure you won't have one?"

Diane shook her head.

"Don't look so glum," said Lydia. "Help is on the way." She downed her drink and reached for the bottle again.

"What help?"

"I dunno. Something."

Diane pursed her lips. "The help you need isn't in that bottle. Get some therapy. Join a support group. You could even go to church."

Lydia laughed. "You're not the first person to suggest that. Remember the minister who did the funeral? He paid a pastoral call to see how I was getting on." She mimicked a preachy voice: 'We must forgive those who sin against us.' I told him where he could stick that."

"Don't talk like that," said Diane. "It isn't healthy."

That night Lydia could not sleep. The photograph of Matthew and Mattie was the last thing she looked at before turning out the light. But when she closed her eyes, the face she saw was that of Mrs. Shaw, tears dribbling down her cheeks. She too must be sleepless tonight. But her loss wouldn't last forever. In a few months, her man would return to her bed. Even now she was not truly alone. In other bedrooms were her other children, and in her womb the one yet to be born.

Would it be a boy or a girl? After two girls, she probably wanted a boy. Or did she care? Would her child be dark like her or fair like Shaw?

Mattie had been like his father. They'd had the same brown eyes and curly hair. Matthew's was black. Mattie's was blond, but would have darkened as he matured.

Lydia turned on the bedside light. Yes, there they were: Mattie on Matthew's shoulders, looking down into his father's face. For the first time she noticed that their radiant smiles were only for each other. Her husband and her son had shut her out. A cold feeling came over her. Would they ever smile for her again?

Drifting into sleep, she heard a baby cry. With desperate urgency she followed the sound through dark and endless corridors. The crying grew louder. The baby waited for her, fled, then waited again. She was getting close. It was right around the next corner. But as soon as she turned the corner, it had moved on. Yet with every step she gained upon it. One more corner and she would have it. She turned the corner, and there was Mattie reaching out to her. She bent to hug him but woke as his arms tightened around her neck.

Lydia sat up and turned on the light. In the framed photograph on her bedside table, Matthew and Mattie smiled.

Outside the window, darkness had paled to the greyish light of early dawn. Too early to rise, too late to get to sleep again. But she had to do something, not just lie there. Lydia swung her legs over the side of the bed. On bare feet she crossed the floor to Matthew's closet.

His clothes—jackets, pants, coats—all hung on the rack just as before. But now they smelled stale, musty and slightly unclean. Strange how completely they had lost the power to stir her. Maybe Diane was right. Maybe this was progress to a further stage. Shock, denial, anger—she'd had them all. But Diane was wrong about acceptance. Lydia saw it now with perfect clarity: the final stage had to be revenge.

One by one, she lifted Matthew's clothes from the rack and stacked them on the bedroom floor. Later, Diane would help to pack them up for the Salvation Army; she'd be delighted to see her sister moving forward.

Emptied of clothes, Matthew's closet seemed spacious. Lydia had forgotten how large it was: four feet by eight. How did that compare with a jail cell? She could keep a captive here. A small captive. A thrill ran through her veins to think of it. An eye for an eye. A tooth for a tooth. A child for a child.

For one crazy minute, she thought it might work. Mattie's baby furniture—crib, changing table, chest of drawers—would fit in here. Diapers, sheets and blankets could go on the closet shelf. The police might search, but they'd find nothing. All she had to do was move the IKEA bookcase from Matthew's study and erect it here to cover the door frame. They wouldn't suspect a second closet in her bedroom.

Yeah, but every time the baby needed a bottle or a diaper change, she'd have to unshelve all the books and move a seven-foot bookcase. And what if the baby cried at the wrong time, like during a police search or when people dropped in? Duct tape? No. This wouldn't work.

But the basic idea was brilliant. Kid snatching happened all the time—non-custodial parents abducting their child. They never got caught. Every month a different notice appeared on the back of her VISA bill envelope: MISSING/DISPARU, case number, date of birth, missing since. A picture taken before the abduction, then a projection of what the child would look like two, five years, ten years later.

For perfect justice, Bill Shaw's child should never be returned. But this was not a perfect world. How long, then? Not ten years, or five, or even two. Too expensive. Too much restriction on her own life. How about six months? Yes. Half a year of sitting in a prison cell not knowing where his child was, whether dead or alive, suffering, starving, or in pain.

Afterwards, she could leave the baby in a basket on the Children's Aid Society steps, or in the women's washroom at the mall. Justice tempered with mercy had a pleasing sound.

With a bunch of flowers in her hand, Lydia roamed the halls of Grace Hospital, checking details like the right kind of ID badge to buy. She noted schedules and mentally charted the best route from the maternity ward to stairways, elevators, washrooms, exits. Fortunately, one hospital handled all the city's maternity cases. Barring some unusual circumstance, this was where Mrs. Shaw would give birth to the killer's child.

There were plenty of ads in the newspaper: "Reliable, responsible woman will give loving care." That's not the woman Lydia needed. "Responsible, reliable" would want an OHIP number. She'd ask questions, and if she didn't like the answers, she'd phone Children's Aid or even the police.

Nor could Lydia place her own ad: "Abductor seeks babysitter for kidnapped newborn." Well, of course she wouldn't say that! But a paid advertisement leaves a trail, and the trail would lead to her.

The ideal caregiver would ask no questions. She'd be someone desperate, marginalized, and not very smart. Downtown were shelters, shop doorways, underpasses, and the mean streets where panhandlers disappeared after the theatre crowd went home. Lydia's search would begin there.

It was snowing, and a couple of inches were already on the ground when Lydia emerged from the underground parking lot onto Wellington Square. Christmas lights twinkled amidst the branches of sidewalk trees and evergreen wreaths hung from lampposts.

Lydia had filled one coat pocket with loonies so she wouldn't have to fish for change in her handbag every time she saw a woman who might do. But for an hour she walked around Wellington Square and up and down Albert Street without success. Where were all the women beggars when she needed one? Lydia's boots leaked and she needed to pee.

Maybe it was time to stop for lunch. After a Big Mac and a washroom break, she'd try the business district. Lydia's fingers closed on the loonies in her pocket.

Then, across the street, Lydia saw a girl huddled near the doorway of the Rendezvous Bar with a gym bag on the sidewalk beside her, mutely lifting her cupped hands to passersby. For the five minutes that Lydia watched, no one dropped a coin. Most passersby seemed not to see her. Everything about her said "beaten dog." Lydia crossed the street.

Close-up, the girl looked like a child decked out for Hallowe'en. Black lips, black-lined eyes, white cheeks. Vampire maiden. So many hoops pierced the outer edge of her right ear that it looked like the coiled spine of a pocket notebook.

Lydia dropped a loonie into her upraised hands. Then another loonie. The girl's green eyes widened. She knew something was up.

"I'm going to have lunch," Lydia said. "Will you join me?"

"Give me a couple more loonies and I'll buy my own."

"No. I want to talk to you."

"You a social worker?" The girls' eyes narrowed.

"Nothing like that. It's just … well, I might have a job that would interest you."

"What kinda job?"

"Taking care of a baby."

"You're looking for a babysitter?"

"Come have lunch at McDonald's. We can talk about it if you're interested."

She screwed up one eye. "I might be."

The girl picked up her gym bag. Standing, she looked smaller and thinner than sitting down. Five-foot-one, ninety pounds was Lydia's guess. About fifteen. Homeless, probably. A girl of the shelters and the streets. Maybe a hooker. But who would pay for that meagre body?

They walked without speaking, side by side through snow that was quickly changing to slush. When they got to McDonald's, the girl paused just inside the entrance while her eyes darted around piercingly, like a animal's looking out through a thicket.

"You're hungry?" Lydia asked.

She nodded.

Lydia bought her a Big Mac, a soft drink, fries, and an apple turnover. The girl devoured the food. Lydia ate a Big Mac, drank a coffee, then went to the washroom. When she returned, the girl had finished.

"What's your name?" she asked.

"Fiona."

"Fiona what?"

"Just Fiona."

A runaway. That was fine. First names were fine. "I'm Lenore," said Lydia. "Just Lenore."

"How old is your baby?"

"Not my baby. I'm helping a friend who's due any day. When her baby is born, she can't take it home or her father will kill her."

"Why doesn't she get it adopted?"

"She wants to keep it. But for now it has to be secret. Next summer, her boyfriend will come for her, and she'll be able to take the baby back."

Fiona looked as if this was perfectly reasonable. "So she needs a babysitter until next summer. Where's the kid going to stay if she can't take it home?"

"Your place."

"You got to be kidding. I don't have a place."

"If you take the job, I'll get you an apartment for six months. I'll supply everything and pay you fifty dollars a day. Cash. But you must be discreet."

"Meaning what?"

"You have to pretend it's your baby."

"Why?"

"No questions. I'm sworn to secrecy. If you have a problem with that, better tell me now."

"No problem."

"Fine. So this is what you have to do: be at the same spot outside the Rendezvous every day between eleven and one o'clock. Twenty bucks a day just to be there. I'll be checking. When the job starts, that's where I'll pick you up."

Mrs. Nagbor's white hair was tied back in a bun. Her cheeks were wrinkled and yellow, and most of the colour had faded from the pupils of her eyes. She spoke little English, barely enough to communicate that Mr. Nagbor, recently deceased, had always looked after finding tenants for the basement apartment in their house. Sitting in Mrs. Nagbor's cramped living room, Lydia nodded understandingly. She would be happy to pay seven hundred dollars per month, first and last in advance. Cash would be fine. And no lease.

The apartment came furnished. Mrs. Nagbor even owned a crib, which she would set up. She had no objection to a single mother with a baby, so long as the rent got paid.

Lydia purchased formula, bottles, diapers, wipes and creams in drugstores where she was not known. Everything went straight to Mrs. Nagbor's basement apartment. The devil was in the details, Lydia reminded herself. If she tripped up, something tiny would be the cause, like a receipt forgotten in a drawer.

She bought a nurse's uniform at The Uniform Shop, white pantyhose at Zellers and walking shoes at Sears. All cash purchases. Nothing to trace.

A cape would work better than a coat, for under it she could wear Mattie's old baby tote. Held snug against her chest, a newborn would be merely a bulge.

Lydia got her shoulder-length blond hair cut short and bought a pair of dark-rimmed dime store glasses. With Lady Clairol's help, she could be brunette in half an hour.

Every couple of days Lydia walked past the Rendezvous Bar between eleven and one. Fiona was always there. She had acquired a baseball cap to hold the money people gave her. Lydia dropped in whatever she owed: forty dollars, sixty dollars, depending on how many days had gone by.

All was in readiness. By now the baby must be due. Each morning Lydia opened the newspaper to the Classified section. No birth announcement yet. Why didn't that damn baby get born? Or maybe it had been born, but Mrs. Shaw had not put in an announcement. That sure would wreck the best of plans. Lydia fretted, bit her nails, and got more nervous every day. And then, on December 5, there it was:

> Shaw. To Bill and Rita, a son, Daren Joseph, seven pounds, six ounces. Born December 4 at Grace Hospital. A brother for Emily and Sara.

Lydia's fingers jittered as she refolded the newspaper. At last the day of reckoning had come. The kitchen clock said 9:00. In two hours Fiona would be at her post, where she would remain until one o'clock. Lydia had plenty of time.

She phoned the hospital.

"Could you tell me Mrs. Rita Shaw's room number, please?"

"Connell Wing, 16E."

After hanging up, Lydia repeated it to herself five times.

Then she went into the bathroom and got out the bottle of semi-permanent, dark brown dye. Comb in, leave on twenty minutes, wash off. Voila! Instant brunette.

Ten minutes to dry and fluff her hair. No time to curl it. She got into her uniform and pinned on her badge. MARGARET MCNEAL, R.N. Very professional. Then she did her makeup: foundation in a slightly darker shade, brown pencil to thicken her brows. The glasses gave a final touch.

Before leaving, she posed in front of her full-length mirror, looking at herself from the front, from over her left shoulder and then from over her right. Perfect. Lydia looked nothing like the sorrowing widow who had read her victim impact statement two months ago in Number One Courtroom.

Matthew and Mattie smiled. They were pleased too. She picked up their photograph and kissed it.

"Wish me luck."

She left her car in the parking lot across the street from the hospital. As she hurried along the sidewalk, her navy blue cape swirled about her ankles. Not so fast! She slowed her pace to a sedate walk. Look calm, she said to herself as she entered the lobby. Look calm yet worried. Pretend you're here to visit a sick friend.

She took the elevator to the basement. This was the tricky bit, leaving her cape and the baby tote in the washroom down the hall from the X-ray department. But this washroom got little use. She had checked that. People needing X-rays didn't make many bathroom stops. Maybe the nurses flushed them out before their journey to the bowels of the hospital.

Lydia hung up her cape and the tote on the hook on the back of the door, then stole a quick look at herself in the mirror over the wash basin. Uniform. Badge. Glasses. She looked like someone you'd trust with your life.

Then up the elevator to the fourth floor. Maternity was down the hall, and then a right turn at the nursing station. The nurses had just carried the babies to their mothers. Perfect timing. Lydia walked purposefully along the corridor, past the premature nursery, where behind a glass wall tiny wrinkled red creatures no bigger than puppies lay in their incubators, naked except for the tubes taped to their bodies. Lydia paused outside 16E, straightened her shoulders, took a deep breath, and marched in.

The ward held four beds. As she entered the ward, four women looked up vaguely with luminous eyes. When Lydia approached Rita Shaw's bed, each of the others returned her attention to the blanketed bundle at her breast.

Lydia smiled. "Sorry, but I need to borrow your baby for half an hour. The doctor has ordered a few routine tests. Nothing to worry about."

"But my baby has been feeding for only five minutes!"

"He can finish when I bring him back. I'll make sure you get extra time with him."

With a soft pop, Mrs. Shaw detached the baby from her teat. The tiny lips continued to suck as Lydia took him into her arms. As she strode out of the ward, she felt Mrs. Shaw's eyes following her.

Left turn towards the elevators, past the nursing station. That was hurdle number one. But the two nurses who sat there continued to work on their charts as she went by. Next hurdle was the elevator, where two orderlies and a nurse waited with an unconscious patient on a stretcher. They all got onto the elevator ahead of Lydia, who squeezed in at one side. At the second floor the others got off. Lydia continued down to the basement.

Carrying the baby openly in her arms, she met no curious glances from the patients who sat waiting in the alcove outside the X-ray room. A white-coated technician who walked towards her, going the opposite direction, nodded briefly.

In the washroom, nothing had been disturbed. She put on the tote, then stuffed the baby into it, blanket and all. A small sigh. Probably he liked it there, dark and warm under the cape, close to her thudding heart.

The extra bulge on her chest was scarcely noticeable as long as she kept her shoulders hunched forward. Lydia took off her glasses, then used the stairs up to the lobby.

The lobby was crowded with people heading this way and that. Just inside the hospital entrance, two uniformed security guards chatted casually. Neither gave her a glance as the automatic door opened and she passed through.

Outside, a middle-aged woman stood beside a man in a wheelchair. A nurse, coatless despite the cold, was with them. A patient going home, Lydia guessed, waiting for his ride.

Twenty feet from the entrance, she passed a huddle of smokers, all leaning towards each other like members of a conspiracy. The two who wore stethoscopes had a particularly furtive air, as if they were even more anxious than Lydia to avoid observation.

She had left her car unlocked—one less thing to fiddle with. And the parking lot had no attendant. Lydia waited while a man got into a Volvo and drove away. Quickly, before anyone else came along, she undid her cape, pulled the baby out of the tote, and laid him on the car floor behind the driver's seat.

The baby whimpered. Probably he was cold, wrapped in one thin hospital blanket. She turned on the car heater full blast. Soothed by the motion of the car, he was asleep in less than the ten minutes it took her to drive home.

She put her car into the garage. With the car door and the garage door closed, no one would hear the baby if he started to cry. It wouldn't be for long—just long enough to shampoo most of the colour from her hair, rinse the shower stall, and shove the nurse's uniform, white shoes, badge, Clairol bottle and all the rest of that stuff into a pillow slip with a brick to weigh it down.

Hurry! Hurry! It was past ten thirty. By now someone must have noticed that Baby Boy Shaw was not with his mother, not having tests, and not in the newborn nursery. The search would be on. The police might already know.

She drove right out of town, heading north through Claxtons Corners and Newburgh until she came to the old bridge where County Road Six crossed the Onondaga River. She stopped on the bridge. There was no other car in sight when she heaved the pillowcase over the railing. The river was deep here, and she was twenty miles from town.

On her way back to the city, Lydia turned on the car radio to drown out the baby's wails. Twelve noon. She switched to the local station for the news. Wars, bombings, robberies. No abductions so far.

Fiona, wrapped in a black leather jacket five sizes too large, sat in her usual place on the sidewalk outside the Rendezvous Bar. When Lydia beckoned from the car, she stuffed her baseball cap into her gym bag and got to her feet. Lydia reached across to open the passenger door.

"Get in."

Fiona heard the wails. "So you got the baby?"

"Yes. He's on the floor in the back."

"That's a funny place to put a baby." Half rising, Fiona twisted in her seat to get a look.

"Sit down, for Pete's sake, and get your seat belt on."

"Afraid the cops will stop us?"

Lydia snapped. "I've better things to spend my money on than traffic fines."

"Then you better slow down. This is a sixty kilometre zone."

She touched her foot to the brake. This was no time to get nervous.

Mrs. Nagbor's basement apartment had its entrance through the side door and down a flight of steps from the landing. The main room, which held a sofa, a coffee table and a television, had a small L-shaped kitchen off the far end. From it one door led to the bathroom and another to the bedroom, where Mrs. Nagbor had set up a wooden crib against the wall opposite the bed.

"Where's the phone?" Fiona asked after her inspection was complete.

"No phone."

"What if you want to call me?"

"I won't."

Lydia ignored the smile that twitched at the corner of Fiona's mouth. "Everything you need is here," she said brusquely. "Food. Formula. Baby supplies. As soon as I leave, you'd better feed him. The instructions are right on the for-mula package." She set the baby on the sofa and opened her purse. "Here's your key to the apartment."

"Okay."

Lydia pulled a fat envelope from her purse. "Here's $1,500 in twenty dollar bills. That's one month's pay in advance. If you need to buy anything, use this money and keep receipts so I can reimburse you."

"When will you be back?"

"In about a month."

"That's a long time."

"I'm going to visit relatives in England over Christmas. You're on your own."

Fiona was counting the money as Lydia left.

On her way home, Lydia stopped at The Bay to do some Christmas shopping. Cardigan for Dad, bath-and-beauty gift basket for Mom, scarf and gloves for Diane. That took an hour.

She was groping for her house key when the unmarked police car pulled into the driveway. Constable Burns and Staff Sergeant Wallace got out.

"What is it?" asked Lydia, careful to express surprise and concern. "Would you like to come in?"

Wallace was gravely polite, bending over backwards not to sound suspicious as she described the abduction of Bill Shaw's baby.

"That's horrible," said Lydia. "One day old! Who could do such a thing?"

The officers wanted to know where Lydia had been all morning.

"I went shopping at The Bay."

"The Bay doesn't open until ten. What were you doing earlier? I'm sorry, but I must ask."

Wallace's soft West Indian voice invited confidence. Lydia saw no threat in the warm brown eyes, yet all at once she felt her breath stick in her throat like an egg she'd swallowed whole.

"I was home, washing my hair."

They said nothing about searching the house, but Lydia knew that would happen sooner or later. She wasn't afraid. The baby had not been here. They would find no evidence of Lydia's purchases or preparation, nothing that could lead them to Fiona or to Mrs. Nagbor's basement apartment.

Lydia spent the next few days addressing Christmas cards and watching the TV news. She surfed the channels to catch Rita Shaw's tearful entreaty over and over again. "Please, please, bring my baby back!" It was on the local news and on the CBC. Even some U.S. newscasts picked it up.

Diane phoned, offered to visit. Lydia turned her down. The company of Matthew and Mattie was all she needed. Once again she felt included in their smiles.

She took the photograph with her when she went to Mom and Dad's place for Christmas. Diane, Joe and the boys were there too, all crowded into the big stone house at Lovatts Corners where Lydia and Diane had grown up.

Everyone pussyfooted around, unsure whether to mention Matthew and Mattie. Lydia overheard their whispered talk. Poor Lydia. The first Christmas after her great loss. How could she bear to sing carols, decorate the tree, smell the savoury odour of roasting turkey?

Diane was the only one to see that, inexplicably, Lydia was coping well.

"You've changed," she said, "since October."

"I guess I was bound to. Like you said, I had to go through all those stages."

Diane looked perplexed. "You don't fit the pattern. Acceptance is a quiet, peaceful state. But you're as tight as a fiddle string." She looked at Lydia reflectively. "May I ask you a personal question?"

"Yes, but I may not answer it."

"Have you ... met someone?"

"Why would you think that?"

"You're so edgy and distracted. Half the time you don't hear when people talk to you."

"So you think I've fallen in love?"

"Well, it does happen. You're young."

Lydia shook her head. Even if she wanted to, she could not have described this new emotion. Excitement, rapture, a touch of fear. Falling in love had felt a bit like that. Or sex for the first time. But she'd never longed for love or sex the way she had longed for revenge.

Lydia didn't think that she was being followed. Yet how could she be sure? The middle of a police investigation was not a safe time to visit Mrs. Nagbor's apartment. But as the weeks went by, and the rent came due, and the advance on Fiona's wages ran out, Lydia had no choice.

The route she took was complex and circuitous. If another car had been trailing hers, she would have seen it long before she drew up in front of Mrs. Nagbor's house. She had the money with her. Her excuse for being late was all prepared.

But Fiona had gone.

"She live here one week," Mrs. Nagbor said, staring for- lornly at her threadbare carpet. "Then she disappear. The baby too. I thought she go home to Momma and never come back. So I got new tenant." Mrs. Nagbor's hands shook; she was trembling throughout her body.

Why, she's afraid, Lydia thought. She thinks she's in trouble because she rented the apartment to someone else after I'd paid two months' rent.

"I give you back the money," Mrs. Nagbor mumbled.

"This is very serious." With an effort, Lydia kept her voice stern and righteous. "You broke the law by taking a new tenant. What's even worse ..." She leaned forward menacingly. "I suspect that your apartment is illegal."

A moan came from Mrs. Nagbor's throat. She pressed her palms together and moved her lips in prayer, or so it appeared, for the words were not English.

"I'll tell you what," said Lydia, "I won't report you. But if the police come, tell them that the girl and the baby were never here. You never saw ..."

Mrs. Nagbor looked up, her pale eyes terrified. "The

police!" she cried as she crossed herself. "I never have trouble before."

Lydia got to her feet. When she reached the doorway, she halted and turned her face towards Mrs. Nagbor.

"Remember. The girl with the baby was never here. Do not say a word."

Lydia did not expect to find Fiona at Wellington Square. Nor had she any idea what she might learn from the youth who huddled on the sidewalk outside the Rendezvous Bar. She didn't recall having seen him before, although she did recognize the black leather jacket, which was as small on him as it had been large on Fiona. Three inches of bare arm showed above his wrists.

"I'm looking for information." When Lydia pulled out a ten dollar bill, the boy's eyes brightened. "There's a girl I want to find. She used to hang out here. Short, very thin. Black lipstick. Black eyeliner. Whole bunch of hoops piercing her right ear. Her name's Fiona."

"Fiona!" The boy laughed.

"That may not be her real name."

"None of us use real names."

"But you do know her? Can you tell me where she is?"

Lydia put the bill into his hand.

"Got another of those?"

"If you tell me."

He looked at her coolly. "The money first." Lydia handed it over.

"She came by here a couple weeks before Christmas.

Said she was going to Vancouver, or maybe San Francisco."

"Alone?"

"Yeah."

"She didn't have a baby with her?"

The youth squinted. "I don't remember."

Lydia pulled out another ten. "Will this help your memory?"

"A couple more will help."

She gave him a twenty. "Okay. Was there a baby?"

"No."

This was like stuffing money into a parking meter. He got fifty bucks from her before she drew the line.

"You get the rest when you've told the whole story. It's worth another fifty bucks to me."

"Not much to tell. She said she'd had a baby, but she'd sold it. A friend of hers looked up private adoptions on the Internet. He posted this baby on the web site. In a couple of weeks this foreign guy showed up and paid her twenty thou for the kid. That's why she had to leave town. There's a law against selling babies, you know."

Lydia gave him the fifty. "What name did she use around here?"

"That's worth another fifty."

"Not to me it isn't." She shut her purse. "Have a good day."

The sun was shining as she drove out of the parking lot under Wellington Square. It was one of those late January thaws, with their false promise of spring in the air.

Time to get on with her life. The price of Matthew's and Mattie's deaths had been paid. Not the full price, but more than she had bargained for. Bill Shaw would never see his child.

The heavy weight of grief had been lifted from her shoulders. What she felt was not quite happiness, but a promise of its possibility. When she got home, she'd phone Diane. If Joe could look after the boys for a week, she'd treat her sister to a holiday in Bermuda. Images of tennis courts and beaches rose in her mind as she drove up Wyandotte Avenue.

Trouble

On my way home from the doctor's, I picked up a dozen eggs at the No Frills down the street from where I lived. I had this room with a hot plate and a microwave. The landlady called it a bachelorette. I shared a bathroom with the tenant who had the other half of the basement.

Next morning, when I cracked the first egg into the frying pan, I seen it had two yolks. That done it. One egg, two yolks. I had to be carrying twins. I was sure of it after I'd finished the whole dozen. Every damn egg had two yolks. How's that for a sign?

That got me thinking about who their father was. I mean, if they turned out to be identical, I'd know they had the same father. Right? But if they're not identical, there was two different sperms. And who's to say whether those sperms would be from the same guy, or not?

I was between boyfriends when I got pregnant. "Between" makes it sound like a gap, as if for a while there wasn't any man in your life. But "between" can be pretty damn crowded. I narrowed it down to Mario and Jerry. It was one or the other, or maybe both, that got me pregnant. I know there are blood tests to prove paternity so you can get child support. But Mario was no more likely than Jerry to make payments. Why bother?

Of course I was going to get rid of them—the twins, I mean. Mario and Jerry had already took off. What changed my mind was my horoscope:

AQUARIUS (January 20 – February 19): Disruption has entered your life. The planets warn that you are tempted to make the wrong decisions. Your birth sign is noted for coming up with ingenious solutions, especially when dealing with changing circumstances. If you put your mind to it, you will find a way to make sense of something that has never made sense before.

That settled it. Your horoscope is one thing you should never fool with. I cut it out from the newspaper and stuck it onto the mirror over my dresser with a piece of scotch tape.

From then on, I found myself thinking about my twins all the time, how at first they were just a few cells, and then they grew little hearts and little spines. It freaked me out to think there were two babies in there, growing eyes and brains and fingers and all.

At first I planned to give them up for adoption. But that sounded like one of those wrong decisions the planets warned about. So I put my mind to it, like the horoscope said I should. I'd go on Mother's Allowance, I decided. That would pay just as good as waitressing at the Sun Restaurant.

Charlie fired me anyway.

"Lynn," he said, "I know you got a problem, but …"

His eyes flitted around looking at everything but my big, round belly.

"But what, Charlie?" I acted like I didn't understand.

He pulled out his wallet and peeled off a fifty. "Here. No hard feelings?"

"Course not." I stuck the fifty into my uniform's pocket, smiled. "Like, who wants to be served by a waitress that looks like the back end of a bus?"

He flushed, starting with his neck, then turning pink right to the top of his bald head. Charlie's married, with two kids nearly grown up. I couldn't figure out why he was so uncomfortable having a pregnant waitress at the Sun Restaurant, which was just a north-end greasy spoon that would be out of business inside a month if anybody opened a Tim Hortons nearby.

Charlie handed me another fifty. "You can come back afterwards. Good luck."

I thanked him for the hundred bucks, went back to my bachelorette and packed all my stuff into two suitcases. It was a good time to move out. I was already two weeks behind in my rent. I waited until I saw the landlady waddle off to the bus stop. She visited her daughter every Wednesday afternoon. This was Wednesday.

I called a cab to the Women's Shelter.

Half of what I said to the social worker was mostly true; the other half was playing along. I figured she knew the ropes and could help me get an apartment and other stuff I needed. But I didn't know how fast everything was going to happen, because one week later, there I was in Maternity Ward.

Twins. I was right. I told a nurse that I knew all along. "Twins," I said. "I knew it. Never had an ultrasound or anything."

"How did you know?"

When I told her about the double-yolk eggs, she smiled and said, "Seriously?"

"You see two babies, don't you? I guess that proves it."

Two babies. Both boys. Identical. So that meant the same father. But whether it was Mario or Jerry I hadn't a clue. Mario was dark, with black hair and brown eyes. Jerry was one of those freckly redheads with green eyes. My little guys didn't look like either. The only person they really looked like was each other. And me, to a certain extent, because they had my mousy hair and blue eyes.

I called one Danny and the other Joey. At first I couldn't tell them apart, unless one of them got a scratch or something. And then I knew one from the other, but not whether the one with the scratch was Danny or Joey.

They both had fat legs and dimpled bums and cute little dicks. I fed those babies, washed them, dressed them. I hadn't had so much fun since Barbie dolls.

Sure, there were bad times too. Single mom. Broke. Nineteen years old. Washing dirty diapers in the bathtub was not fun. I couldn't afford the disposable kind.

But it was all worth it when I watched them sleeping, one at each end of the crib, and felt my heart just about burst.

By the time they were six months old, I could see a difference in their personalities. Danny was a do'er, active like. Joey seemed content to lay there staring at his fingers. When they were old enough to hang onto things, I got them both rattles. Danny would shake his as hard as he could. But Joey jiggled his, sometimes holding it to his ear as if trying to figure out what made the noise inside.

When they started JK, I shortened their names to Dan and Joe. I didn't want them to have baby names when they started school, especially since they were small for their age. They looked like they were three years old, not four.

I was afraid the other kids might pick on them, but that didn't happen. They got along fine, even though they didn't make other friends. Their teacher, Mrs. Withers, said that was their own choice. They didn't want or need any friend except each other.

Mrs. Withers tried splitting them up. She put Dan with the bluebirds and Joe with the chickadees. But one of them was always sneaking away from his own group to be with the other. Mrs. Withers didn't force it. She said she'd been teaching kindergarten and JK for twenty years and she'd seen all this before.

"They were once the same egg," she said to me at Parent-Teacher's Night. "I think identical twins carry that through life."

A month later she phoned to ask me to come and see her.

"What's the problem?" I asked.

"Oh, no problem. Joe and Dan never cause a problem. There's just something I want to talk to you about."

I was back working at the Sun Restaurant by then, so we had to find a time when it wasn't my shift. I brought the boys with me, to save the cost of a sitter. They looked at books in the Story Corner while Mrs. Withers talked to me. I was sitting on one of those little kiddie chairs, and she had pulled up another to sit facing me, our knees bumping. She had nice eyes and a big smile. I could see why Joe and Dan loved her.

"You have two wonderful children," she said. "They're both self-confident. They're poised. They have a lot of presence."

"They have?" I said.

Then she got to the point. Her husband was with the opera company. They were going to put on an opera about this American guy who goes to Japan and gets married to this geisha girl, Madame Butterfly. He doesn't think they're really married, but she does. She has a little boy. Mrs. Withers wants Dan and Joe to play that part.

"Both of them?" I asked. "It sounded like one little boy."

"Just one. His name is Trouble."

That definitely was a sign, but my mind was filled with so many questions that I didn't notice.

"The director wants both boys for the role," she said, "so they can take turns. There'll be four performances every week for the whole month of February. That will be too tiring for one little boy. Besides, if one gets sick, the other can stand in for him."

When Mrs. Withers said how she would pick them up, and stay with them, and bring them home afterwards, I thought, well, why not? So I said that she could ask them if they wanted to do it. And they said that they did.

Dan and Joe were right at home on stage. All they really had to do was look cute and wave an American flag. I saw two performances. Free tickets. I took Dan to see Joe, and Joe to see Dan. The audience ooed and ahhed for them both. They had black wigs with tiny pigtails, and a beautiful silk costume that they shared. I thought the opera company might let them keep it, but it had to go back to some outfit called Malabar's.

After the final performance, Dan and Joe each got a copy of the cast picture and some photos showing them on stage. I got a big bunch of roses just for being their mom.

I didn't think any more about it until one morning I heard singing from the boys' bedroom before they got up. One of them was singing a song that Madame Butterfly sings in the opera: "Un bel dee ve-dromo le var see un fill dee fumo." Anyway, that's what it sounded like. It was in Italian, so I don't know what it means.

"Which one of you was singing?" I asked at breakfast.

"It was Joe," said Dan.

Joe looked embarrassed.

"Will you sing it for me?" I asked.

So he did. He stood with his hand on his heart and sang like a bird.

"Now let's hear you too," I said to Dan.

But he shook his head. "I can't."

"Oh, go on," I said.

He tried, but he was right. It sounded like nothing. I was amazed. I always thought that anything one could do, the other could too.

It didn't take Mrs. Withers long to discover that Joe could sing real good. The school was having a spring concert, and she got him out there doing the whole song. The audience went wild.

That was just the beginning. There were more school concerts, talent shows, Kinsmen Club musicals. Joe never had to audition; directors came looking for him. By the time he was eight, he'd been in *The King and I, The Music Man and South Pacific*. I never had to take him to rehearsals. Some nice lady always picked him up and brought him home.

I sometimes wondered what the nice ladies thought, coming out to Trafalgar Heights low-cost housing, where they had to shoulder past punks doing drug deals in the hall. The place was a hellhole. But it didn't bother Joe and Dan.

There were some bad kids at Trafalgar Heights. I saw them smoking in the corridors, smashing the playground equipment that the Rotary Club had just put up. Stuff like that. Older kids used the littler ones for shoplifting and B & E's because they were too young to get charged as Young Offenders.

Of course I worried about my boys getting caught up in that kind of stuff, but after a while I seen it wasn't likely to happen. Peer pressure didn't exist for my boys. A lot had changed since they were in JK, but they still didn't have or need any friends except each other.

Whatever made Joe happy, made Dan happy too. The same happiness kinda flowed through them both. One day I seen my reflection in the mirror, and the thought came to me real sudden: that's just like Joe and Dan. Joe smiles, Dan smiles. Joe cries, Dan cries. Know what I mean?

That's terrible, I thought. Dan's got to have something special of his own. He didn't have a musical bone in his body, so it couldn't be music. So I asked him if there was anything he'd like to take up, like a sport or hobby. Me all the time crossing my fingers so he wouldn't say hockey. I couldn't afford that.

Quick as a flash, Dan said, "Karate."

"No kidding?"

He said it so fast I figured he'd been thinking about it already but maybe didn't think there was any point asking.

"Right," I said. "We'll find out where you can take lessons."

"At the Y. A kid in my class goes there."

When I told Charlie that Dan wanted to take karate, he shook his head.

"How old is he?"

"Eight."

"Well, I dunno. Would you give a gun to an eight year old?"

"What are you getting at?" I said.

"I heard a guy with a black belt got convicted for assault with a deadly weapon when he beat somebody up with his bare hands. You sure Dan's mature enough? You don't want him knocking the block off some kid in the schoolyard."

"Geez," I said, "you sound like I'm raising a pit bull, not a little boy."

"Just warning you."

All the same, I thought I'd better check the horoscope before I let Dan start. Charlie always picks up a copy of the newspaper for the restaurant. I grabbed it soon as I got to work the next day. My horoscope didn't say much—no warning of any problem. But then it occurred to me it was Dan's horoscope, not mine, I should be checking. It was Joe's too, of course:

PISCES (February 19 – March 20): Try to open your mind to unusual thinking. As a result, you might want to head in a new direction. Investigate what you need to do. Sign up for a class or workshop. Consider a trip that might also be educational. Tonight: follow the music.

I read it over two, three times. It blew my mind, how this horoscope covered both boys. There was Dan wanting to sign up for karate classes, and Joe following his music.

Dan needed a uniform called a Gi. It was like big, floppy white pyjamas. Fifty dollars seemed a lot, but it fit so loose I figured he could get a couple of years out of it before he grew too big. I had to buy him a white belt too (another twenty bucks).

It started off okay. Dan practised his karate on Joe, who didn't mind Dan flipping him around the living room. Dan tried it on me just one time. That was after he'd moved up to Orange Belt. I landed flat on my back on the kitchen floor. "No thanks," I said. "You can save that for your brother."

The twins were moving in separate directions now, but they were just as close as ever. I sometimes used to think my boys were like two sides of the same coin. But that was wrong, because Dan and Joe looked the same as each other. To help the teacher tell them apart, they didn't wear identical clothes. But the shirt that was on Joe one day could be on Dan the next, or at least as soon as I got it washed.

Dan went with me to Joe's musicals, and Joe went with me to Dan's karate exams, where the kids showed how they were ready to get their next belt. The belts were like grades at school. White was like Grade One. After that came Yellow, Orange, Green, Blue, Brown and Black.

After he got his Green Belt, I said to Dan, "Don't you worry about hurting somebody or getting hurt?"

"Nah," he said. "Of course I could kill somebody if I wanted to. But karate isn't about killing people. It's about discipline and being the best you can be."

"Oh," I said. "That's good."

But the idea he could kill somebody gave me a jolt.

The trouble started at the cast party for *Oliver*. At least, I think that's when it started. Over at the refreshment table, Joe was loading his plate with frosted brownies and Nanaimo bars, like he always did at receptions. Before a performance either he couldn't eat or didn't like to.

Joe was Oliver—his first starring role. He had his picture in the paper. Big time! He was just eleven, which was why I got included in the party.

I noticed the man standing beside Joe at the refreshment table. It was hard not to notice him, because he looked like a penguin. None of the other guys were wearing tuxedos, so I figured he'd been to some other event—maybe a concert—before coming here. He hadn't been part of the production, so either he'd crashed or somebody else had brought him along. He had short legs and a big belly. He even waddled like a penguin. I watched him follow Joe to the chairs that were along the walls, and sit down beside him.

The man held a glass of white wine in his hand, but I didn't see him raise it to his mouth. He was talking, talking all the time. Joe listened, his head cocked slightly to one side. Between bites of brownie and Nanaimo bar, he glanced up and nodded.

I took a real long look. There was something about the way the guy leaned toward Joe.

Joe's eyes searched the room. When they met mine, he smiled and looked relieved. Maybe he needed me to rescue him. And whatever that guy was telling Joe, I ought to hear it too. I walked over. The man stood up politely and held out his hand, which was soft and sweaty.

"How do you do, Mrs. Grady?" (I wasn't a Mrs., but that didn't matter). "I've been having a fascinating conversation with your extremely talented son."

"Yeah, I see that." I felt like grabbing Joe and dragging him out of there. But Joe's eyes were wide and shiny, and he had a big grin pasted across his face.

"Mom, guess what?"

I didn't have to guess. Joe's new friend handed me a business card: DR. ANDREW PHINEAS. CHOIR MASTER. ST. SWITHIN'S CHURCH.

While I was reading the card, he said, "Joe and I were discussing his future. His voice is too precious to waste on musical theatre." He laughed, as if the idea of musical theatre was too silly to be taken seriously. "He has also reached the stage where he needs vocal training. Talent isn't enough, you know. Without proper training, he could ruin his voice. With it, he may become one of the great boy sopranos of our age."

Joe's eyes shone. Who wouldn't be flattered? Like, if some talent scout came up to me and said that I could be the next Julia Roberts, I'd be over the moon.

"What's it going to cost?" I asked, thinking how minimum wage wouldn't pay for many voice lessons.

"Nothing. St. Swithin's boy choristers receive a first rate musical education at no cost. Not only that, but the church pays them a stipend of twenty dollars per week, rising to thirty at twelve years of age."

At this, Joe was jumping up and down, grinning at me with all his teeth.

"So what does he have to do?" I felt suspicious already.

"Sing three services every Sunday and attend choir practice twice a week."

"Can I, Mom? Can I? Can I?"

"Sure," I said, "if you like."

I managed to get to one service every Sunday, depending on my work schedule. I didn't care much for the music. Some of the hymns were okay, but there was too much classical stuff. Joe loved it, though.

I find most churches kind of creepy, but this one was beautiful, with a high arched ceiling that had angels painted on the plaster between the beams, and tall stained glass windows with Bible story pictures, and a long centre aisle called a nave. There was a parade down the nave at the start of every service, with the choir and some priests and a couple of people carrying candles and a cross.

The choirboys had to wear a long red robe partly covered by a white thing called a surplice. And there was this frill they all wore around their neck. I couldn't believe any normal boy would be caught dead in a getup like that.

Dr. Phineas had told the truth about the vocal training. It wasn't just choir practice. He gave Joe a private lesson every week.

I had to wash and iron Joe's surplice whenever it got dirty. I took the surplice and Dan's Gi down to the laundry room with the rest of our clothes. The surplice reminded me of a nightgown, and the Gi of pyjamas. Both were weird.

A couple of months passed. Joe was so full of these great stories about the choir—how famous it was and how many countries it had visited on tour. He was old enough to take the bus from Trafalgar Heights right downtown to St. Swithin's. Either Dr. Phineas or one of the Choir Mothers drove him home. When he turned twelve, his pay went up. Then they made him Head Chorister, which added another ten.

One day when I was ironing his surplice it occurred to me that I spent more time with this damn surplice than I did with Joe. Dan and me hardly saw him any more. When he wasn't at school, he was doing something with the choir. They had concerts as well as Sunday services. And when they weren't practising or performing, they were having parties, hikes, picnics, sleigh rides. In the summer, the whole bunch went to Choir Camp. Depending on the season, there was always something. Like, it took over Joe's whole life.

I was sad for Dan. When I went to see him get his Blue Belt, Joe couldn't go with me because of Saturday morning choir practice. But you should have seen Dan whip those guys through the air! It was like that Chinese movie about crouching tigers and hidden dragons. Dan rented the video so Joe and I could watch it with him, except that Joe wasn't home.

One Saturday morning, while we were eating breakfast before Joe left for choir practice, I asked him, "Don't you miss being in those musicals?"

"Sometimes." Joe took a bite of Cheerios. "I don't think about it very much."

I noticed that he was blinking. He never did that before, blink real fast, and sometimes a twitch in his cheek. Nervous like.

"There's auditions coming up for *Annie*. Maybe they got a part for a boy."

"In *Annie*? I don't think so." He pushed his cereal bowl away. "Even if there was, I couldn't do it. Dr. Phineas won't let us be in anything else." He gulped his milk and ran to catch the bus.

Did Dr. Phineas think he owned my boy? That choir was turning Joe into a slave. Why did he do it? Loyalty? The money? Yeah, probably. Forty dollars a week was a big deal. So was being Head Chorister. But Joe wasn't a happy boy any longer. He was getting plenty of attention, but I could see he wasn't having fun.

I had the ironing board set up in front of the TV and was pressing Joe's surplice. Dan was watching *Creepy Canada*, and I had half an eye on it too, when Joe came in. He'd been to choir practice.

"Mom, can you get me a passport?" That question came right out of the blue, before he even took his coat off.

"What do you need a passport for?"

"The choir's been invited to sing in Germany. We're going to a whole bunch of churches." His eyes were blinking. Danger signal.

"Who's paying?"

"St. Swithin's is having a fundraiser. The choir boys have to pay nine hundred dollars each, except for me."

"Why, except for you?"

"Everybody knows you can't afford it."

"Why didn't Dr. Phineas talk to me about this first?"

"Because he never sees you."

"He could have phoned."

Joe fixed his eyes on the carpet. "I'm Head Chorister, so I have to go."

"No," I said. "You can't go free if everybody else has to pay."

Silence. I was holding my breath, keeping my anger in.

"Are you mad at me?" Joe asked.

A smell of scorching. I didn't realize I was pressing so hard. When I lifted the iron, I seen that the white surplice had the shape of my iron burned right into it.

"Goddamnit! Look what you made me do!"

Joe crammed his fists into his pockets. Dan, sitting on the sofa, twiddled his thumbs furiously.

"Mom, Dr. Phineas says I have to go." Joe's voice shook. I turned off the iron.

"So … do you do everything Dr. Phineas tells you?"

"Yes." He started to bawl and charged out of the room.

Dan ran after him into their bedroom. The door closed. I heard Dan talking, Joe crying, Dan talking, Joe blowing his nose.

I took the surplice into the kitchen to see what I could do about the scorch. It was yellow, not brown. Maybe Javex could take it out.

The walls are thin in these low-cost apartments. I could hear the boys talking and talking, their voices muffled like conspirators. A year ago I couldn't have told which one was speaking, but now I could. Those voice lessons had somehow carried over into Joe's ordinary talk. But I didn't know what they were saying. It was just between the two of them.

I remembered what their JK teacher Mrs. Withers had said, years ago: "They were once the same egg. I think identical twins carry that through life."

The talk in the bedroom went on and on.

Suddenly Joe yelled, "No! You promised you wouldn't."

Scuffling sounds. Something crashed. Then a thud. I raced to the bedroom, opened the door. There was Joe flat on his back, staring straight up. Dan, leaning over him, slowly twined his fingers and said to me, real calm, "Don't worry, Mom. Joe's not hurt."

"What is it you promised not to do?"

He shot me a furious look. "Tell you what's been going on. What Dr. Phineas does to him."

"What Dr. Phineas does to him?"

It hit me then. A bolt that flashed in front of my eyes and shot to the top of my head. God! What a blind idiot I'd been.

"Yeah," said Dan. "That's how he got to be Head Chorister."

I had to sit down. It took me a good five minutes before I could get my breath. Then I went into the bedroom to hug Joe and tell him I loved him.

After that, Joe quit the choir. He kept away from St. Swithin's, stayed home in the evenings.

St. Swithin's Choir had to cancel their trip. They couldn't very well go on tour without a choirmaster. It was a tragedy what happened to Dr. Phineas, to break his neck in the choir room. I heard that he had stayed late, as he often did, after choir practice. Probably he had climbed onto a chair to take down some sheet music from the top shelf. When the verger found him, there was an overturned chair and sheet music all over the floor.

Dan had been late coming home from karate class that night.

Acknowledgements

I would like to thank:

My publisher: Maureen Whyte at Seraphim Editions for taking a chance on a new author.

My editor: Kerry Schooley.

Janice Jackson for her artwork. Marijke Friesen for the design.

Chris Pannell, Director of the New Writing Workshop, and also everyone at the workshop who helped with criticism and suggestions.

My first circle of readers: Linda Helson, Barbara Ledger, and Debbie Welland of the Creative Writing Group of the Hamilton Branch of the Canadian Federation of University Women.

My friends and family, especially Janet Myers, Karen Baxter, Alison Baxter Lean, and finally my husband John for giving me space to write.

The following journals and anthologies for previously publishing selected stories: *Lichen Literary Journal*, *Other Voices*, *Hammered Out*, *Canadian Writer's Journal*, *Hard Boiled Love*, and *Revenge*.